# The Kid Who Got Zapped Through Time

# The Kid Who
# Got Zapped
# Through Time

## Deborah Scott

AVON BOOKS  NEW YORK

• • • • • •

*AVON BOOKS*
A division of
The Hearst Corporation
1350 Avenue of the Americas
New York, New York 10019

Copyright © 1997 by Deborah Scott
Interior design by Kellan Peck
Visit our website at **http://AvonBooks.com**
ISBN: 0-380-97356-1

Library of Congress Cataloging in Publication Data:

Scott, Deborah.
The kid who got zapped through time / Deborah Scott.—1st ed.
p.    cm.
Summary: When Flattop Kincaid buys a used video game at a flea market, he finds himself in the Middle Ages among peasants who think he is a deranged member of the nobility.
[1. Time travel—Fiction. 2. Middle Ages—Fiction.] I. Title.
PZ7.S4175Ki  1997                         97-440
[Fic]—DC21                                CIP

First Avon Books Printing: September 1997

## For the kids in the
## Torrance and Tehachapi School Districts

## ACKNOWLEDGMENTS

History isn't just about names and dates, it's about *people* who did the best they could with the information they had. While the characters and places in this book are fictional, they represent the lifestyles, customs, and beliefs of the people who lived in many parts of Great Britain in 1150 A.D.

*I would like to thank the following people for their help:*

Members of the Society for Creative Anachronism and other "Living History" reenactors who answered all my questions.

My critique partners for keeping me on my toes.

My friend and cohort, Marti Schwartz, who instilled in me the *chutzpah* to find a publisher.

Senior Editor Gwen Montgomery, and all the wonderful professionals at Avon Books, who have made this a fantastic experience.

*And special thanks to my family:*

My grandmother, who read to me whenever I asked.

My mother, who showed me the magic of libraries.

My father, who never doubted for one instant that I could do anything I wanted to.

My brother, whose indomitable spirit *is* Flattop Kincaid.

My husband, David Hall, who is my partner, my inspiration, and my greatest teacher.

## FLATTOP KINCAID
### Saturday, May 5

The name's Flattop Kincaid, Adventurer Extraordinaire. Ordinarily I wouldn't be able to write stuff like "extraordinaire," but I have this spell checker on my computer that lets me write the word the way it sounds, then spells it right. My parents bought the software at the swap meet. I wanted "Starfighter 207." They wanted me to pass English.

I had to hear a bunch of stuff about my potential and how my life would be ruined if I didn't get down to business and study, study, study. I think they said something about Harvard in there someplace—they usually do. And all this time, the swap meet guy is standing there going, "Kid, do you want this Starfighter or not?" I tell you, it's getting more and more embarrassing to go anywhere with my parents.

They're nice enough people and everything, but they can get on my nerves. My mom, Eleanor, used to be a cheerleader. Now she just kind of whines, you know? Not really whining, but when I ask if I can go with my friends to a BMX bike jump, she scrunches up her face like her shoes hurt and says,

"Ohhhh, I don't think that's such a good idea. You could really hurt yourself, Marvin."

Yeah. Marvin. Do you believe a kid could get named Marvin? I had a great-grandfather named Marvin, so my parents thought it would be nice for me to have the same name. There's something to be said for kids picking their own names. I would've picked a good one like Jason or Josh. That's what a lot of the boys at my school are named.

Anyway, when I started sixth grade at Thomas Jefferson Middle School last year, I got a haircut that made my hair stand up on my head. My dad says they used to call it a "flattop." Well, I thought it sounded like a cool name, because it says who I am.

My dad says when he was my age, his friends called him "Stretch." Duh. Could that be because he was six foot four in the seventh grade? His real name is Daniel. His mom named him that because of the lion's den in the Bible. Even that's better than the great-grandfather thing.

My dad's a little more understanding about guy stuff, but he still doesn't go for bike jumping. He says, "When I was your age, we took good care of our bikes." And he's not crazy about video games, either. "When I was your age, we went outside and had our own adventures." But I'm not allowed to do anything adventurous.

I don't get any help from my sister, Marcia, either. She's in high school now, so she thinks she's grown up and can boss me around more than ever. When my mom says I can't do something, Marcia's always there to say, "Mom's right, Marvin. You're too young to understand it right now." Like she's lived. She comes home from school, talks on the phone all night, then goes to bed. The boyfriends she gets are a regular dweeb-a-thon. But she knows best. Oh yeah.

So you see, things can get pretty exasperating around my house. (I just used my spell checker to write exasperating. I guess I like it. It did get me better grades.) But what I really

**want is excitement. I want "Starfighter 207." And today I'm going to get it.**

---

With that, Flattop Kincaid saved his journal entry and turned off his computer. He checked his watch, then frantically searched through a pile of dirty clothes, pulling out a crumpled envelope. Inside was forty-five dollars, mostly in one-dollar bills. That envelope represented six weeks of mowing lawns, walking dogs, recycling soda cans and cleaning the neighbor's garage. All for "Starfighter 207," the adventure of a lifetime.

During the ride to the swap meet, Flattop sat in the back seat in a flood of bright May sunshine. He counted his money at least ten times while his parents talked about boring adult stuff in the front seat. When they pulled into the parking lot, he jammed the roll of money deep into his pocket. As he walked through the entrance to the booths, Flattop Kincaid smiled and said to himself, *Life is perfect.*

"Life stinks," Flattop grumbled, two hours later. He had walked down every aisle at the swap meet and the software guy wasn't there. *Figures,* he thought.

He was mad at his parents for ruining his life, so he told them he'd meet them at the popcorn stand in an hour. He wanted to be alone. Besides, his dad was comparing prices on running shoes and his mom was in one of those booths where they sell fake designer perfumes. If disappointment didn't kill him, boredom would.

He walked down to the far end of the last aisle and saw an empty booth under a tree. Flattop wandered over to investigate. Behind the long empty table was a bright blue plastic curtain held up by a metal frame. An old man came out from behind the curtain and walked up to the table. His fingers were bony and twisted and he held onto a walking stick that was taller than he was. His face was thin and he

3

had a long white beard. Flattop thought he looked like one of those magic guys who wears a pointy hat and robe, except this one wore a jogging suit.

"Looking for software, are you?" the old man asked.

"Yeah," Flattop said. "You got 'Starfighter 207'?"

The old man's face wrinkled up in a smile. "I've got something much better." He reached through the back curtain and pulled out a game box Flattop had never seen before. "Do you like 'Dungeons and Dragons'?"

"Yeah, but I was looking for 'Starfight—'"

"Silence, my boy. You're not looking for a starfighter, you're looking for an adventure, right?"

Flattop shrugged. "Yeah."

The old man held up the box. It sparkled as if it were catching sunlight, even though they were in the shade. "This is what you have been searching for all your life," he said.

"Can I see it?" Flattop asked.

"Of course." The old man held the box at Flattop's eye level.

"I mean, on a computer."

"I don't have one."

Flattop smiled. "Well, how do I know what the game is like?"

The old man got very serious. He clenched his fist and stepped toward Flattop. "This is no game," he whispered. "This is reality!"

Flattop wasn't exactly scared, but he was nervous. He shoved his hands into the pockets of his jeans and rocked back and forth on his heels. "How much does it cost?"

"How much do you have?"

"Nothing." After all, he wasn't sure he wanted it.

The old man shook his head. "There's no such thing as a free ride, Marvin, my boy."

Flattop's mouth dropped open. *How did he know my name?*

"Or should I call you Flattop?"

4

Flattop stepped back and looked him over. "How do you know my name?"

"I know many things, my dear boy, least of all your name. And I know that you must have this adventure. So pay me the forty-three dollars and forty-nine cents you would have paid for 'Starfighter' and be on your way."

" 'Starfighter' was only thirty-nine ninety-nine."

"Plus tax."

Normally, Flattop was pretty cool under pressure, but this old guy had him kind of shook up. He handed over the money and the man gave him the game box.

"The instructions are in the software. Follow them very carefully," he added, cautioning Flattop.

As Flattop walked back to the popcorn stand, he was flooded with questions. What if the game didn't work? Could he bring it back? That's when he realized he hadn't gotten a receipt. Flattop ran back to the tree where the old guy had his booth, but he was gone—completely gone. There was no sign that a table, a plastic curtain or the old man had ever been there.

Flattop felt kind of sick and dizzy, so he hurried back to the snack stand to get a blue raspberry Icee. How could a whole booth just disappear? Maybe he was seeing things. Little kids with really high fevers see things. He pressed his hand against his forehead. No fever.

He sat on a bench in the shade sipping his Icee. His parents were already fifteen minutes late. He watched the sweet, blue liquid drain from the ice with each pull on the straw. If *he* showed up late, he got a lecture on responsibility.

When he saw them hurrying toward him he considered asking where they'd been, but he knew he'd get a lecture on respect for his elders. Besides, they'd be mad enough when they found out he spent all his money and didn't get a receipt.

The ride home was unusually quiet. Normally, Flattop bugged his parents to change the radio to another rock station every time a commercial came on. But he was staring out the window, so lost in his thoughts that he didn't care about the radio at all—which was probably a good thing, because his parents were listening to an oldies station and happily singing "Elinor G" with the Turtles.

When the song was over, his mom turned around and patted him on the knee. "You okay?"

"Huh? Yeah." He went back to staring.

"Did you have a good day?" his mom persisted.

Suddenly it occurred to Flattop that the conversation was getting dangerously close to *Show us what you bought.* He had to think fast.

"The sun's really bright today, huh?" he said, cringing inside. He hated to be put on the spot like this. He saw his dad exchange a glance with his mom. Any minute now, they were going to ask what he'd bought. He'd have to try something bold and daring. He'd have to take a chance.

"Did you get any perfume at that place?" Flattop asked. It was a gutsy move because it involved both the topics of

6

purchases *and* the swap meet, but he had to give it a try. Luckily, his mom went for the bait.

"No," she said in her disgusted-mom tone. "That place had more expensive stuff than all the other booths put together. It's terrible, the way they . . ."

He had succeeded. She was busy complaining about the price of perfume. Next, his dad would gripe about the cost of running shoes. Flattop had managed to steer the conversation away from the software he'd bought that had no name, no printed packaging and no receipt. As he settled back contentedly, his dad's words crashed in on him. "Did you get your game?"

*No fair! You can't just jump in with a question like that!* Flattop stalled for time. "Huh?"

"Did you buy that game you wanted?" his dad said, a little slower.

"They didn't have it, so I bought another one," Flattop mumbled.

"Which one did you get?" his mom asked.

*Oh great, now they're ganging up on me.* He continued to look out the window, pretending not to care. "Just another adventure one. I've never played it before, but I hear it's really good."

He hadn't exactly lied. The old man told him it was good.

The rest of the trip went pretty smoothly. Ol' Eleanor and Dan sang along to a Beatles double play. Flattop rested his head on the retractor for the back seat belt. Every bump knocked the plastic cover into his temple, but he didn't care. He was thinking about the old guy at the swap meet and the $43.49 he'd spent.

When they pulled into the driveway of their house, Flattop ran inside, game in hand. In a matter of seconds, he'd be safe in his room—a sanctuary from nosy parents. As he shut the door, he felt the small knot in his stomach finally loosen.

He pulled the disc out of its plastic case to get a better look, and found something else in there, too. It was a mirror—sort of—but the glass was a deep, dark purple-y black. You really had to strain to see your reflection in it, but if you needed a mirror, it would do. It was about the same size as a wallet photo, so Flattop could stick it in his pocket.

*Great. If nothing else, I've got a forty-three dollar and forty-nine cent mirror.* He turned on his computer. The monitor displayed a waving hand while the audio played "Stars and Stripes Forever." Flattop smiled proudly. It'd taken him three days of his spring break to program that. He reached for the unmarked game disc and held his breath as he loaded it into the computer.

The sound of flutes played a classical melody and a title filled the screen:

## Days and Knights
## Adventures for the Third Millennium

He looked up the word *millennium*. "A thousand years," he recited from the dictionary. "So the third millennium is the third thousand years. What's that supposed to mean?" he muttered, as he idly flipped the dictionary pages with his fingers.

"Flattop. Flattop," came a vaguely familiar voice. Flattop looked toward his bedroom door, waiting for his grandfather or Mr. Gardner from down the street to walk in.

"Pssst! Over here, Marvin, my boy." The voice was coming from his computer. There on the screen was the familiar figure of the strange old man from the swap meet. He was dressed in a long, flowing purple robe and a cone-shaped purple hat.

"You!" Flattop gasped.

"Good, my boy." The old man raised his arm to cheer Flattop's powers of recognition.

8

"I knew you looked like one of those guys," Flattop said. "Those . . . what do you call 'em?"

"Wizards?" offered the old man.

"Yeah! That's it!" Flattop was triumphant. "Wizards! I knew you looked like a wizard!" He jumped up from his desk and gave a loud whoop of victory. "Yeah! Wizards! Awright!"

Just then, there was a knock on his door and his mother peeked in to find him in mid-celebration in the center of his bedroom.

"What's going on?" she asked.

"Where?" Flattop said, stalling.

"Here." His mother seemed amused and curious, a dangerous combination.

*Think! Gotta think!* "Nothing." He shrugged.

"What was the hollering about?"

"Oh . . . nothing." Flattop looked down at his shoes and noticed one of his laces was untied. "I just . . . you know . . . nothing."

"Well, you've got twenty minutes to get to Pizza World for Jason's party."

"Who?"

Flattop's mother stepped all the way through the door now. "Jason. Your friend? His birthday party is at six o'clock, remember? Let's get moving." She closed the bedroom door on her way out.

That's right. Jason Lane's birthday party was tonight. A pizza party and a sleepover with four other boys in Jason's backyard. They had planned this for weeks. Flattop turned toward the computer to find the Wizard standing silently. Suddenly he didn't want to go to Pizza World, or Jason's house or anywhere. He wanted to play the Wizard's game.

"Maybe I can get in a couple minutes," he mumbled.

"Sorry, Marvin, my boy," the Wizard said sincerely. "An

adventure takes more than *a couple minutes.* We'll play tomorrow."

"No," Flattop protested. "I can play for a little while." But the computer screen went blank and the game disc popped out all by itself. When he tried to insert it again, it wouldn't budge. "Hmmm."

"Marvin, honey," his mom called, "Dad's waiting."

He didn't have time to investigate this now. He quickly shoved the disc into his top desk drawer. He picked up the purple-y black glass and turned it over and over in his hands.

"Marvin!" his dad barked. "Let's get moving!"

"Okay," he replied.

Flattop threw the glass into the desk drawer, flicked the computer power switch and turned the monitor off. He stood motionless as he heard the whirring of the hard drive come to a stop. As though a spell had been broken, he quickly dove into his closet, grabbed his sleeping bag, a pair of sweats and his comb, and lunged toward the bedroom door. Stopping suddenly, he reached into the top desk drawer, retrieved the dark glass, then rushed out to the car.

It was about midnight, after they had eaten four large pepperoni pizzas, six bowls of popcorn and a bakery birthday cake, when the boys settled into the large tent in the backyard.

"Look at the moon, you guys." Jason pointed at the sky. "That dark part right in the middle. It's a zebra, kind of."

"You're blind," Sean said, wriggling toward the tent door in his sleeping bag. "That's an eye. See how it's almost across from the other eye?"

"What do you think, Flattop?" Jason asked.

"Huh?" Flattop hated to be the deciding vote.

"What does that spot on the moon look like?"

Flattop studied it carefully. "Ms. Hogue."

The boys doubled over with laughter at the mere mention of "Haggy" Hogue, the assistant principal at their old elementary school whose hair stuck out as if she had been electrocuted or something. They laughed over that one for a good ten minutes.

Then they decided it would be cool to go to the moon and find out that the shadows really were the actual face of some horrible outer space monster who'd been spying on Earth for centuries.

11

These theories were slowly replaced with the relaxed, steady breathing of six tired boys who were stuffed with junk food. Flattop took one last sleepy glance at the full moon and slowly closed his eyes. In the next split second they popped open again, and a frightening realization clenched at his gut. That game had called him by name. How was that possible? It must've been programmed in the software. But how would the old guy have known that Flattop was going to buy that disc? Then he remembered the old man had called him by name at the swap meet—even called him Marvin. This sat uneasily on top of all the pizza and birthday cake frosting. He reached into the corner of the tent where his jeans were crumpled in a pile and took out the dark glass from one of the pockets. With the light from the full moon overhead he could almost make out his reflection.

*I wonder what this is for?* he asked himself over and over as he rubbed his fingers along the rounded corners and smooth surface. Deciding to think about all this later, he rolled over on his side and closed his eyes.

He woke up several times that night, in the middle of dreams about wizards and knights running around on his computer screen. The whole thing had him puzzled. At about five o'clock in the morning, he gazed wearily into the dark glass and watched the reflection of the retreating moon through the branches of the pepper tree in Jason's backyard.

What was the game like? Maybe jousting. Yeah, jousting would be good. Or you could help Sir Lancelot kill a dragon and save a fair maiden. That's pretty typical knight stuff. Or defend truth and justice in a battle with the evil Black Knight. Maybe the object of the game was to go on a quest. Everyone knows that's the kind of stuff knights lived for.

He sighed, tucked the glass back into his jeans and rolled over on his grumbling stomach. Eventually it would be time to go home and find out what the game was really like. He smiled to himself, pleased with the number of interesting possibilities he had come up with. Maybe he should design computer games when he grew up.

The next time he woke up it was nine o'clock, when Jason accidentally kicked him in the face trying to get out of the tent. The smell of frying bacon had drifted out of the kitchen, and the boys were powerless against its spell. They straggled out of the tent and into the house.

Breakfast of bacon and French toast started out quietly enough, but the powdered sugar and maple syrup soon had everyone talking at the same time, laughing loudly and kicking each other under the table. The boys were all on the same Little League team and, with May being just about mid-season, the competition among the teams was heating up. This afternoon their very own Red Sox would be playing the Giants. They argued and gossiped about the Giants' best pitcher while Jason's mom cleared the table and loaded the dishwasher.

While this kind of talk was usually pretty entertaining, Flattop had gotten a lot less sleep than his friends and just wanted to get home to his computer. He was so quiet during breakfast that Mrs. Lane asked if he was feeling all right. He assured her everything was fine and tried to act a little more hyper for her benefit. At ten o'clock he combed his hair, changed his clothes and headed for home, making sure he thanked Mrs. Lane for the nice party.

He got home, had the usual conversation with his parents about how the party was, then went to his room, explaining that he hadn't gotten much sleep. He watched his mom and dad trade knowing glances before he disappeared down the hall and into his room. Shutting the door, he looked at his computer and took a deep breath. Whatever was going on with this game, he was going to get to the bottom of it.

He reached into his hip pocket and pulled out the glass, then sat in his chair and flicked a couple of switches. The

13

computer was up and humming. He punched past the waving-hand graphic and the "Stars and Stripes Forever." He inserted the game disc and carefully studied the screen. There were the flutes again, playing the classical music. Then the title:

# Days and Knights
## Adventures for the Third Millennium

"Yeah, yeah," Flattop muttered impatiently. "Get on with it."

"Hold your horses, Flattop, my boy," came the Wizard's reply. "We have to satisfy our marketing department with a proper opening."

Flattop, cranky from too little sleep, grumbled, "Well, I don't have all day. Tell me how you got my name on the game disc."

The Wizard smiled back from the monitor screen. "Planning. There's a valuable lesson in always being prepared."

Flattop was tired, but he could still tell that the Wizard was avoiding the question. "You didn't answer me. Is this some new laser technology?"

The Wizard frowned. "You're taking this far too seriously."

"Are you going to tell me how you did it?"

"No."

"Oh." Flattop hadn't been prepared for an out-and-out refusal.

"Marvin, when you came to me, you wanted excitement, thrills, something different—not a lesson on laser technology. Now, my question to you is, are you ready for an adventure?"

"Yeah, I guess so."

"Then hold on to the dark glass and follow me!"

With that, the Wizard on the monitor screen turned his back and ran. After a couple of steps, the graphic on the screen showed him breaking through the stark black background as though it were made of construction paper. On the other side of this background was a beautiful green countryside with rolling hills and a thick forest. In the distance was a small thatched-roof hut.

"This looks like England or something," Flattop mumbled.

The Wizard looked back at Flattop. "Smart boy. Now come on."

"Wait!" called Flattop. "You didn't tell me how to play the game!"

"Just follow me!" came the far off cry.

Flattop watched the Wizard disappear over the last hill. He pushed a couple of keys: "enter" key, "arrow" keys. Maybe that would advance the picture. But nothing moved, not even a leaf on one of the trees in the distant woods. He wiggled the dark glass across the glowing monitor screen. Maybe it reflected something. No luck. He sat staring at the picture of the countryside for a good five minutes.

He heaved an angry sigh. "Well, that does it. I got cheated."

His mother knocked softly then opened the door. "I thought you'd be asleep."

"No," was all the reply he could muster.

"Well, it's time to get ready for your baseball game," she said in a hushed voice.

Flattop sat a moment longer, staring at the blank monitor screen, then nodded. "Yeah, I guess," he said as he turned off the computer.

While his mom went to the kitchen to fill a thermos jug with cold water, Flattop changed into his Red Sox uniform. Mr. Hartman, his Little League coach, had the boys go through a dressing ceremony before each game. Flattop felt

**15**

pretty stupid doing it, but the Red Sox had won every game since they started it.

Pulling the white T-shirt with the long, bright red sleeves over his head, he recited, "Red sleeves mean a Red Sox player has powerful arms."

He quickly rolled calf-length tube socks up his legs. "White makes my steps sure and true."

He pulled the dark stirrup socks over each foot. "A Red Sox player is fast of foot." He never understood why he had to say it that way, but Mr. Hartman made them memorize the whole speech, word for word.

He rocked back on his bed and pulled the white pants over both legs at the same time. He stood up and tugged at the zipper, then ran his thumbs along the red stripes on the outside seams. "Red stripes mean a Red Sox player has strong legs."

Tossing the gold V neck jersey over his head and wrestling both arms into the sleeves, he held his hand over the red satin letters that spelled *RED SOX* across his chest. "Red means Red Sox players have *miles and miles and miles* of heart." His dad told him that Mr. Hartman had stolen that line from a play about baseball.

He stood before his full-length mirror and tucked in his shirt. Mr. Hartman had given them gold uniform shirts instead of the usual white ones. He said there were lots of other teams named Red Sox, but this made them one of a kind.

Flattop studied his reflection in the mirror, then put on his prized red satin jacket. It would be good to get some baseball in. Maybe it would take his mind off crooked old guys who were just out to steal a kid's money.

He put on his red cap, saying, "Red means a Red Sox player outthinks his opponents." Then he gave himself a last approving look, grabbed his cleats and headed out the door.

The Red Sox/Giants game was such an easy victory, it

was kind of embarrassing. The Red Sox took a fifteen-run lead in the first inning and never lost it. Without any Giants hitting down the line or threatening to score, Flattop was pretty bored playing third base. He couldn't keep his mind from wandering. He thought about what it would be like to go back to the swap meet and tell the old guy off. Then he realized something. *Why go all the way back to the swap meet? I'll just turn on my computer and yell at him there.*

Flattop gasped. He felt his knees get rubbery. It hadn't occurred to him until just this minute. He'd had a conversation with the Wizard that morning. There were no printed instructions on the screen—just the Wizard. And when Flattop had asked a question, the Wizard had answered it. This situation had gone past being weird. He knew he could never tell anyone what had happened, for fear they'd lock him away someplace.

The loud crack of the bat brought him to his senses, but it was too late for him to catch the line drive that zoomed by, two feet above his head. Luckily the left fielder moved in and snagged it on the fly, ending the game. The coach normally would've yelled at Flattop, but instead looked at him and said, "You don't look so hot." Flattop weakly shook his head.

When Flattop didn't jump around and throw his mitt in the air to celebrate the win, his parents were concerned that he was sick. On the way home, they turned the radio off and talked in quiet voices. As they pulled into the garage, his mother said, "You go right in and lie down. I'll make you some soup. Maybe you need something a little more nutritious than all the sugar and starch you've had for the last twenty-four hours."

Flattop nodded and trudged into the house. His mom must be worried. She didn't even yell for him to take off his cleats before going inside. Once he was in his room, he closed the door and shuffled over to the bed. He sat down for a minute, then gazed at the computer. *Just one more time.*

He turned it on. Flutes, title, and finally the Wizard. "Flattop, my boy, I thought you wanted adventure."

"I do, but you ran away."

"If it's adventure you seek, you must come with me."

"I don't know how. You didn't tell me how to work the stupid controls and—"

The Wizard's voice was soft and he spoke in a measured tone. "If you want the adventure, you must come with me."

Flattop paused and swallowed hard. "How?"

"Pick up the glass," instructed the Wizard.

Flattop snatched up the glass with an impatient sigh.

The Wizard lifted his hand up to the computer screen and held it there. "Now, touch the glass to my hand."

Flattop hesitated, wiped the sweat and dirt off his right palm, then clutched the glass and placed it on the monitor over the image of the Wizard's hand.

What could only be described as frightening purple flashes of lightning streaked through Flattop's brain—that, and the thought that he'd just electrocuted himself. A loud thudding sound pounded in his head. It was his heartbeat, and it was getting louder and faster by the second. He tried to shut the computer off, but his hands jerked and shook uncontrollably. He gasped for breath and tried to stand up, but his body felt like Jell-O.

*Oh great, I just killed myself,* was Flattop Kincaid's last thought before everything went black.

# 4

The first thing Flattop felt was cold. Wet cold. And he smelled smoke, like the time his dad had started a fire in the fireplace and had forgotten to open the flue. For a second he panicked, because he couldn't see anything. Then he realized his eyes were closed. He didn't want to open them because he knew that something horrible had happened when he touched the glass to the computer screen. Something scary. Something that was all his fault. And he didn't care to see what it was.

Lying there with his eyes closed, he tried to figure out what happened. He came up with two possibilities—either the computer had blown up in his face and he'd been rushed to a hospital where a team of surgeons was preparing to operate on him, or the entire house had blown up and rescuers were still sifting through the wreckage for survivors. Feeling cold and wet and smelling the faint scent of chimney smoke overhead, Flattop decided that the second choice made more sense.

It was the whispering that finally aroused his curiosity. Tiny, frightened whispers from two—no—three voices. He decided to open his eyes. It took most of his strength and

19

concentration to raise his eyelids, but when he did, he saw three raggedy children—two girls and a boy—peering down at him.

"He lives!" the little boy shouted, stepping back.

Flattop's eyes focused on the boy first. He wore a hood that looked like part of a Halloween costume, and a baggy, moth-eaten wool tunic tied with a rope belt. Underneath, he wore brown wool pants that made him look like he'd stepped into the sleeves of a sweater. His nose was runny, and his dirty, matted hair poked out of his hood and stuck to his forehead.

The boy stooped to touch Flattop's jacket, but the older girl grabbed him by the arm. "No, George!" she ordered.

"What shall we do, Margaret?" asked the other girl.

The older one thought for a moment, then turned to the boy. "George, you must fetch Father. Catherine and I will stay here."

"Yes, Margaret." The little boy nodded and took off running.

*Catherine? Margaret? George?* Flattop didn't remember any kids on his block with those names. And they had accents— English accents. He studied the two girls. They couldn't be more than first- or second-graders. They wore long tunics, two or three layers thick, with old linen aprons on top. A few wisps of dark brown hair had come loose from their head scarves and flopped across their dirty faces.

*They must've been playing "dress-up" when the explosion happened,* Flattop reasoned.

It was then he realized the cold, wet feeling was the damp ground underneath him. There was no bedroom floor, no sidewalk, no street. Where was his chair, his computer, and the charred remains of his three-bedroom, two-bath house with family room? For that matter, where was his family?

*Oh no! I blew up the whole neighborhood!*

He wanted to speak, but couldn't get his mouth to form

the words. It took every bit of strength he had to raise his head an inch off the ground. As he did, the two girls gasped and jumped back in fright.

"He will get us!" screamed Catherine.

Margaret picked up a rock and held it menacingly overhead. "Mind yourself, sir. I am not afraid of you."

Flattop managed to shake his head and half-whisper, "I'm sorry." Then he drifted back to sleep.

He was roused a second time by something prodding his ribs.

"Come on, lad," a gruff voice urged. "Up with you."

For an instant Flattop thought his dad was trying to get him up for school. He waited for the familiar, "You don't want to be late," then realized it wasn't his dad's voice. He opened his eyes a little quicker this time. It seemed the extra sleep had helped. A thin man stood over him. His tattered brown hat cast a dark shadow over much of his face. Only the dark brown tip of his beard caught the afternoon sunlight.

Flattop propped himself up on his elbows to look around. "What's going on?" There was no sign of his house—just miles and miles of empty, green hills and that smoky smell again. A surge of panic raced through his stomach and up to his heart, making it pound furiously.

"Where is everything? Where's my house?" he asked, trying frantically to sit up. A dizzy spell stopped him. Flattop closed his eyes and grabbed his head. He felt a pair of hands support his back. They were small hands, but strong. He could tell by the way the fingers sunk into his shoulders as he struggled to sit up.

"There now, boy, have a rest. 'Tis a lot you have been through." A woman's voice—young, but rough around the edges—rang in Flattop's ears. He turned around to get a look at her. Her skin was tan and leathery, but she looked like the three children who were huddled behind her.

"Are those your kids? Where's my mom and dad? What am I doing here? Who are you?" The questions spilled out. The woman raised her head to exchange a worried look with the man.

"Somebody tell me what's going on," Flattop pleaded.

The man wiped his brow with his thick, woolen sleeve. "I am called John. This is my wife, Ruth. 'Twas our children who found you."

John looked toward the distant woods, then took his hat off and ran his hand along the brim. Flattop studied his face. Thin and drawn, it was the face of someone who was probably a lot younger than he looked. His dark hair, like the young boy's, was a tangle of sweat and dirt. Though his shoulders and chest were lean, it was obvious—even through the layers of worn-out tunics and sweaters—that there was strength and stamina in them. His big hands were a map of cuts and bruises, and his thick fingernails were black with dirt.

The man sighed, as though forced to do an unpleasant task, and began to speak. "You see, lad, as near as we figure it, you and your parents were passing through Lord Hemstead's forest."

"What forest?" Flattop protested. "We weren't in any forest."

"Easy, boy." The woman rubbed his back. "We think you have been hurt."

Flattop looked down at his body to check. He was still in his baseball uniform, red satin jacket and all. Then a sequence of half-thoughts raced through his mind: *Uniform . . . baseball . . . house . . . computer . . . wizard.* "The Wizard!" Flattop shouted. "He told me to follow him! He said to take his hand!"

"Who?" asked John.

"That wizard guy. I was in my bedroom. He told me to follow him!"

The woman looked at the man. "I am afraid he is bad off, John. Very bad."

"Now, son." The man shook his head. "You have had a frightful experience. We do not have much, but we will share it with you while you are mending."

Flattop looked around with new energy. "Where'd the Wizard go?"

The man grabbed Flattop's shoulders and looked him straight in the eye. "Boy! Listen to me. We will give you a roof and share our bread, but you cannot talk like the devil himself has gotten into you! You will do best to be silent about such things as wizards."

Flattop's brain was going ninety miles an hour, trying to make the pieces of this strange puzzle fit. Once before, he'd felt this way in a dream. That was it! This was a dream. Everybody knows dreams don't have to make sense, so he decided to play along.

"Okay, you win. I won't say anything about the . . . that guy I just mentioned." He looked into John's eyes and saw not only concern, but fear. He cleared his throat and continued, "What do *you* think happened to me?"

"Well, lad," said the man, "you and your parents were on the way to Lord Hemstead's castle when you passed through his forest. Everyone in these parts knows that the Robber King has claimed the woods for himself."

"Who's Robert King?" Flattop asked.

"No," the woman corrected. "Robber. The Robber King."

The man shook his head. "He is a vile man. Lord Hemstead has sent his finest men into the woods to capture the thief, but each one ends up with his throat slit or his head caved in."

"Then, how did I get away?" Flattop was beginning to like this dream. It had adventure in it.

The man paused and cleared his throat. "We figure he killed your parents, gave you a good bash on the head, then left you to die."

Flattop had never had a dream in which his parents died. It sent an icy tingle down his spine. The woman saw him shiver and said to her husband, "He has taken a chill. We must get him inside."

John nodded. "Aye, Ruth."

In the next instant Flattop found himself gathered up in John's arms and carried toward a little thatched-roof hut about fifty yards away. The fact that John was only a little taller than Flattop made the embarrassment of being carried like a baby even greater. Secondly, he realized it was the man's clothes and hair that smelled of chimney smoke. He turned away to look at the strangely familiar surroundings: English countryside, rolling hills, small hut, dense woods. Where had he seen this before?

He gasped in recognition. "My game! I'm in my game!"

Fifty yards went by fast when Mr. Hartman had the baseball team do wind sprints, but fifty yards was a long way to be carried like a baby.

"That's okay, John." Flattop struggled in the man's grasp. "I can walk."

"No!" Ruth said. "He is hurt."

"I know that, woman!" the man scolded as he tightened his hold. "Margaret?"

"Yes, Father?" The oldest girl ran to John's side.

"Prepare a place for the lad to rest."

"Yes, Father." The girl raced to the hut and disappeared through the open doorway.

In an instant, three chickens scurried out the front door, clucking and flapping their wings.

*This must be some kind of little barn or something,* Flattop thought to himself. *I thought it was their house.*

Just as he was about to be carried through the door, two squealing pigs darted out, slamming into John's shins.

"Oomph!" The man's knees buckled.

"John! Be careful!" Ruth shouted.

They stumbled in through the doorway and John lowered Flattop to his feet.

"Here, Father, I made a bed for him." Margaret pointed to a bundle of straw near a feeding trough.

"That's okay, I don't need to lie down. I—"

"Nonsense, boy, you are hurt. You must rest while my wife sees to your care."

Flattop looked quickly around the room for a better place to lie down, but found only hard, wet dirt sprinkled with chicken and pig droppings. Maybe the pile of straw wasn't so bad after all.

He eased himself down, bunching handfuls of straw in some places and smoothing out lumps in others. When he looked up, he was surprised to see the entire family leaning over him, watching his every move.

"It's nice." He forced a polite smile. "Thank you."

Ruth thrust a wooden bowl at him. "Drink this. It will clear your head."

Flattop raised the bowl to his mouth and sipped cautiously. The mixture smelled rotten and tasted worse. He couldn't help wincing as a shiver ran down his spine. It took a minute for his saliva glands to settle down before he could ask, "What is this?"

"Sour mash," the woman answered proudly. "It's good for you. Drink up."

Suddenly the small wooden bowl looked bigger than the one-gallon Tupperware pitcher his mom made Kool-Aid in. His mind quickly reviewed the list of excuses he used when he didn't want to eat something. "I'm allergic," he announced triumphantly. The man and woman looked at each other, puzzled. "Allergic," Flattop repeated. "I have an allergy. When I drink this stuff, I get a really bad rash. It lasts for a week."

Ruth's expression brightened. "Oh! I can make a tea of ground earthworms for that. Children, fetch me three—"

"No!" Flattop shouted, startling everyone including himself. "That's okay. I'll take my chances with this stuff." Bracing himself, he lifted the bowl and gulped down the liquid in four big swallows. His whole body shuddered and he couldn't catch his breath. He quickly wiped his watering eyes on the sleeve of his jacket. He tried to croak out a polite, "Thanks," but his vocal cords were burning. Come to think of it, his stomach was burning, too.

"Now, lad, you just lie there and let the medicine work." John gently pushed Flattop's shoulders back onto the pile of straw. Flattop nodded in surrender. This couldn't be a dream. *People in dreams don't make a guy go through all this,* he reasoned.

He looked closely at his surroundings for the first time. The dirt-floor hut was a little bigger than his family room at home. The walls and ceiling were a mixture of mud, straw and sticks, and it looked hard as cement. There were no windows, and the doorway didn't have a door. The only other opening was at the highest point in the roof, where a jagged hole let in the late afternoon sunlight.

In the center of the floor were the smoldering remains of a fire. Three tree limbs came to a point over the ashes and were tied at the top, tepee-style. This formed a holder for a black pot. Ruth took a big stick and sifted through the ashes. She sprinkled a handful of dried moss over the top and carefully blew on it until the moss caught fire. Slowly she added twigs, then bigger pieces of wood, until healthy flames sizzled under the pot. Flattop watched most of the smoke curl around the black kettle and escape through the hole in the roof. The rest lingered, forming a gray cloud in the room. *No wonder everyone smells like smoke.*

Catherine and George swept the chicken and pig droppings out the door, raked through the straw on Flattop's side of the room, then ran outside. Flattop felt a little fuzzy-brained—not really sleepy, but not really awake. *These people live in a barn?* he asked himself. Hearing a couple of swishes, he turned again to see Ruth using her apron to brush chicken droppings off the dinner table. At least, he guessed it was the table, even though it was nothing more than wooden planks nailed together and placed on top of what appeared to be two saw horses.

Flattop pushed up the sleeve on his prized red satin jacket to look at his watch. It was a little hard to read because he was seeing double, but finally he made out the numbers. Four o'clock in the afternoon.

"How are you feeling, boy?" Ruth had noticed him stirring.

"My eyes aren't seeing so good," Flattop said, rubbing his forehead, "and my head feels funny."

"That's the medicine, lad," was the last thing he heard before falling asleep.

## • • • • • •
# 6

A terrible squeal jolted Flattop awake. John had chased the two pigs into the room, and they didn't like it one bit. In fact, they were hysterical, oinking and racing around the room in circles. The kids ran in next, shooing three chickens through the door.

Flattop sat up quickly, then felt an awful pounding in the center of his brain.

"Owww!" he moaned, as he grabbed his head.

"Anything wrong, lad?" John asked.

"My head." Flattop grimaced. "It's killing me."

Ruth bent over him, then touched her rough hands to his forehead. "No fever. That is good. The medicine is working." She stood up and wiped her hands on the front of her tunic. "Are you ready to take supper with us, then?"

He remembered his mom was going to fix him a sandwich for lunch, but that had been hours—or years—ago. "Sure. I'm kinda' starved." He sat up slowly, wondering if he was ever going to make sense of all this. That's when he saw the little boy carefully inspecting the dark purple glass the Wizard had included in the computer game. "Hey! What are you doing with that?" Flattop shouted as he struggled to his feet. All activity in the room stopped.

"He's got my thing!" Flattop charged. "My glass thing!"

"I found it!" George replied.

"You took it! That's mine!" Flattop was standing over the boy with his hands clenched into fists. He was ready to bop the little creep on the head if he didn't get that glass back *pronto*.

" 'Tis mine now!" yelled the boy.

"No, it is not." John stepped between them, then turned to Flattop.

"Begging your pardon, lad," he said in a nervous rush. "My son is only a small child and does not know what he has done. It was never his intent to take what is yours. Please forgive him. He is young."

"It *is* mine," Flattop restated.

"I am sure it is." John wrenched it from the little boy's hand without even looking at him. "I beg of you, please do not hold this mistake against the child, or against any member of this family." He handed the dark glass to Flattop, who stuck it in the pocket of his baseball pants.

"Thanks," Flattop mumbled as he looked at the dirt floor. He was embarrassed at the big scene he had made. If he acted that way with one of his little cousins, one of the adults would've said, "Oh, Marvin, it's just a silly piece of glass. Stop making such a fuss." But it wasn't just a silly piece of glass. For all he knew, it was the key that could get him out of this weird mess and help him find the Wizard— wherever he was.

After a long silence, Ruth cleared her throat and said, "Well then, let us make ready for supper." Everyone nodded and went to work pulling bowls out of a wooden chest and arranging seats around the large, square table.

There were only three handmade stools, so John tipped a wooden box on end to make a fourth seat. Flattop helped

Ruth move the big wooden chest to the table, so it could serve as a bench seat for two more. John motioned for Flattop to take one of the stools. "Here lad, make yourself comfortable."

But Flattop remembered that at big Thanksgiving dinners at home, it was his duty to sit on the piano bench with his sister, so he sat on the wooden chest with Margaret. A steaming glop of stuff that looked like oatmeal was spooned from the kettle into six roughly carved wooden bowls. Catherine brought them to the table. "Thank you," Flattop remembered to say.

They bowed their heads to say grace, just like Flattop's family did on holidays like Thanksgiving. While John gave thanks for their "bounty of food," Flattop noticed that the glop in the bowls smelled like Cream Of Wheat. When John asked God to "bless this food," Flattop looked at his folded hands. They were filthy—like everyone else's. *Mom would never let me come to the table looking like this.*

There was an "Amen," and, just like Thanksgiving at his house, everybody grabbed for the food. Flattop looked for a spoon, then saw everyone else pick up the bowls and slurp the stuff right into their mouths. He remembered trying that trick at a restaurant once and getting the lecture of his life.

But no one seemed to mind it here, so he picked up the bowl and started slurping. The glop even tasted a lot like Cream of Wheat without all the sugar and milk he usually added. Maybe it was a little more bitter, but he was too hungry to be picky.

Flattop wiped his mouth with the back of his dirty hand. "That was pretty good. What was it?"

John and Ruth looked at each other. They seemed surprised he didn't know.

"Porridge," Ruth replied.

"Porridge? Real porridge? You mean like *Goldilocks and the Three Bears?* That's cool."

Ruth stood up and reached for his bowl. "If it has cooled, I shall heat it again."

"No." Flattop grabbed the bowl. "It's hot, it's hot. *Cool* means that it's . . . cool. You know . . . good."

John rubbed his beard. "And do they say this *cool* where you come from?"

"Yeah."

"Yeah?" John tried out this second new word.

Flattop had a teacher once who wouldn't allow him to say *yeah,* so he corrected his obvious mistake. "I mean, yes, sir."

"Do you remember anything else about your homeland?" John asked, speaking very slowly.

"Sure. I remember lots of stuff."

Ruth grabbed John's hand. "The medicine is working."

John continued, "Do you remember what you are called?"

"Yeah. Flattop. Everybody calls me that."

John beamed at his wife. "Yeah Flattop."

"Yeah Flattop." Ruth beamed back.

"No, just—not *Yeah Flattop.* Just . . . Flattop."

Margaret repeated, "Flattop."

Catherine and George giggled. "Flattop."

For an awkward moment they all seemed to be happily staring at the glop in their bowls. Flattop made a stab at continuing the conversation. "You have cute kids."

John looked puzzled. "Kids?"

"You know," Flattop explained, "children."

"Oh, I see." John smiled. "Yes, we have produced five children, three of which you see here." He gestured toward the girl seated beside Flattop. "That one is called Margaret. She is our eldest daughter."

"Good day," Margaret said, suddenly blushing.

"Margaret has seen seven winters," John added, then nodded to the other girl. "This one is called Catherine. She has been with us six winters."

The *winter* thing confused Flattop at first, till he figured out that was how they counted years. *Six winters means six years, give or take a season or two,* he guessed.

"Hi, Catherine." Flattop smiled.

Catherine put her hands to her face to stifle a giggle.

"Our boy," John continued, "is George. But his mother and I call him Little George. He has seen four winters."

"Hi, George."

George buried his head in his mother's lap.

"Where are the other two?" Flattop asked, pleased that he was doing such a good job at dinner table chitchat.

"The other two?"

"Children," Flattop said. "You told me you have five."

A hush fell over the table.

"They are with God," John said softly. "We lost our oldest boy in his twelfth summer."

"And the youngest boy died this winter of—" Ruth's voice caught in mid-sentence. She cleared her throat and continued, "—of the fever."

Flattop felt like a total jerk. Everything was going along just fine till he had to ask about the rest of the kids. Why couldn't he learn to leave well enough alone?

"I'm sorry," he mumbled. "I didn't mean to ask you about anybody who was . . . you know . . . dead." He felt his cheeks flush with humiliation, and the anger he directed at himself made his body heat up. Without looking up, he struggled out of his red satin baseball jacket and let it slump around him.

John pointed to Flattop's uniform. "The figures on your shirt. They are the same as the ones on the back of your overgarment and on your hat."

Flattop looked down at his gold shirt. It said *RED SOX.* So did the jacket. And his hat had the initials *RS* on the front. "This is my uniform—for my team. Everybody wears this."

33

"It is an unusual coat of arms," John said. "You all do battle under the same name?"

"Yeah. We're the Red Sox."

"From where do you hail, lad?"

Flattop remembered hearing this in an old Robin Hood movie, so he was back on familiar ground. "I hail from L.A."

"And . . . is that in France?" John asked.

"No," Flattop said, laughing. "L.A." When he saw that everyone at the table looked confused, he added, "You know . . . in California."

Ruth stood up to clear the bowls from the table. "It must be far away."

*It must be,* Flattop thought.

## 7

"Would you care for a drink, Flattop?" John motioned to Ruth, who scurried from the table to get three wooden cups and a hammered metal jug.

Flattop shuddered to think what might be in the jug. "I'll just have water," he said quickly.

"My goodness, lad! The water is not fit to drink." Ruth poured a tan-colored liquid from the jug and shoved it in front of him. "Have a taste of ale."

The only thing Flattop knew about ale was that you had to be twenty-one to drink it. But he was thirsty, so he grabbed the wooden cup and took a sip. A strong scent of apples filled his nose and the sweet flavor made his taste buds jump for joy. At last, something he recognized! "Hey," he said, laughing. "It's cider. I love cider." He gulped the rest of his drink while John and Ruth shared theirs with the children. *If ale is just apple cider,* he thought to himself, *I wonder why you have to be twenty-one to drink it?*

John let out a satisfied sigh. "Well, the sun is set, and we are to bed." The whole family stood up. Flattop scrambled to his feet. Ruth collected the dirty bowls and scraped the leftovers back into the cauldron. Flattop thought about all the germs from dirty hands and mouths that had just been put back into the big pot of porridge. Margaret opened the top of the wooden chest she and Flattop had been using as a seat and placed the dirty cups and bowls inside. Flattop stared, openmouthed. Even when he and his dad went camping, they made *some* effort to wash the dishes.

Catherine and George pulled the stools and boxes away from the table and, with Flattop's help, lined them against the wall. Hearing a couple of grunts and a loud "oomph," Flattop looked toward the table to find that John and Ruth had thrown a large mattress on top. He joined the rest of the family as they pushed, patted and fluffed it into place. The material that covered it was rough, and by the way the insides rustled, he guessed it was stuffed with straw.

One by one, the whole family disappeared out the door and went separate ways. Where were they going? To another house? To other beds? Was that big bed for him? No one had said a word. Flattop stood at the door and watched John take Little George to the river. There was just enough light left that he could see them stand by the water's edge and take down their pants.

While John shot a yellow stream into the river, Little George squatted beside him. Flattop gasped in shock. He took a step outside the doorway, to see if anyone else was watching. George and John were now busily grabbing handfuls of grass to use on George's behind. Even when Flattop went camping, he'd always used one of those little sheds his dad called a one-holer. And they always had toilet paper. He swore an oath—right on the spot—that he would not go to the bathroom until he got home. Whenever that was. Wherever that was.

Margaret and Catherine skipped around the corner of the hut. That's when he realized this was family bathroom time. Girls went one way, boys went the other. It didn't matter—it was still disgusting. John and George returned to the hut at the same time Ruth did. John looked at Flattop then motioned toward the river. "Are you sure you do not need to—"

"No thanks," Flattop said weakly. *I'd rather hold it until I explode,* he added, to himself.

John leaned a heavy piece of scrap wood across the doorway, then patted Flattop on the shoulder. "To bed with you, son." All Flattop could think about was, *Is that the hand he used to help George out by the river?*

He watched the entire family climb atop the table and pull what looked like a ratty old horse blanket on top of them. Assuming his bed was the pile of straw, he turned toward it—only to find that it was the pigs' bed, now. "Flattop, come on, lad," John said with a hint of impatience in his voice. "We cannot wait all night."

He had never seen a whole family sleep together on top of a table before, but since he had no family of his own right now, the idea was comforting, in a weird sort of way. He took off his satin jacket and crawled up onto the edge of the table next to George. Ruth tossed the blanket over him. It had a musty farm smell to it and made a little poof of dust when it landed on him. A blast of stale body odors invaded his nose. The boys' locker room at his sister's high school didn't smell this bad. Getting to sleep might not be so easy.

When Flattop closed his eyes, a dozen mental pictures flashed through his brain. His bed at home. His mom always coming in to say good night. His dad sharing a tent with him on fishing trips. He hadn't realized how much his parents took care of him and watched over him.

When he spent a week at baseball camp, his parents took him to the chartered bus and helped load his duffle bag into the luggage compartment. Then they stood outside until the bus left. He could see them still waving good-bye as the bus turned the corner. And even though he didn't see them for a whole week, they wrote him every day.

Flattop rubbed his fingernail along the rough material of

the blanket. Now he was all alone in a strange place with strange, stinky people. Even the Wizard had deserted him. He listened to the steady breathing of John's family.

*Alone.*

He'd have to stay with John and Ruth until he found out how to get home. But he knew how to mind his manners and he really wouldn't be any trouble. A couple more glops of porridge certainly wouldn't make them go broke. It wasn't like he was eating steak and lobster. He'd just have to remember to say please and thank you all the time. Flattop smiled to himself, happy that he had a plan of action. Before long, the heavy blanket and the family lying close together made him feel warm and cozy, and he fell asleep.

In the dark of night, Flattop awoke with an unmistakable pressure on his bladder. This happened a lot when he went camping, too. He tried to lie perfectly still and hoped he could go back to sleep. That's when he heard John and Ruth whispering.

"But the boy is not ours," Ruth said.

"No one has come looking for him."

"How do you expect to feed him when we cannot feed the children we have?"

"He can help us," John insisted. "He is older, stronger, well fed and—"

"He is from a noble family," Ruth interrupted. "Very rich. You have seen his red satin overgarment as well as I."

"We need his strength in the fields and he needs a home."

"What if someone comes for him? What if they see him working the fields?"

"We shall tell them we have cared for the lad as best we know how," John answered in a matter-of-fact voice.

"They will say we stole the boy. They could have us put to death." Ruth's voice was choked with fear.

"If we do not use his help with the planting this year, we may all die of hunger come next winter." John paused when he heard Ruth sniffle. "Woman, we have lost our son and this boy has lost his parents. God has given us each other."

Ruth sighed. "He is a very kind boy, for a noble. Maybe he *is* a gift from God."

The words swam in Flattop's head. *We cannot feed the children we have.* Flattop felt his newly formed plan of action crumbling before he'd ever gotten a chance to use it. He'd assumed John and Ruth would take care of him. He'd assumed they'd feed him. But they didn't have enough food for their own kids.

*Gift from God. Use his help.* Not only were they in no position to help him, but they hoped *he'd* help *them.* Fear clutched at his stomach. How could he help them? He was just a kid.

*Red satin. Noble family. Put to death.* They thought he was rich because of his jacket. They were afraid they'd be killed if they helped him. And still, they'd decided to take him in. Even if they had to risk their lives. Even if they had to starve.

Flattop furrowed his brow. They were doing all of this because of him. He felt embarrassed and stupid and unworthy. And very alone.

His eyes stung as tears rolled across his cheeks and onto the straw mattress. Part of him wanted to hear what else they had to say and part of him knew his heart would bust wide open if he did. He clenched his teeth to fight back the sob that was building in his throat. With a long, slow sniff, he acted like he was just waking up. John and Ruth *shushed* each other. Moving his sleeve across his eyes, he rubbed the tears away from his face, making it look like he was stretching.

He had to go to the bathroom anyway, so he would use that as his excuse to go outside and put himself back together again. He sat up slowly, keeping his back to John and Ruth.

"What is it, lad?" John whispered.

"I gotta go to the . . . you know . . . river."

"Aye, lad. Do you need someone to—"

"No," Flattop said quickly. "I can go by myself. No problem." With that, he eased himself down off the table. Realizing for the first time that the temperature was pretty chilly, he grabbed his jacket and squeezed out around the big piece of scrap wood that was propped across the doorway.

As he made his way to the river, he filled his lungs with the cold night air and began to feel better. A couple of snaps and a zipper later, he was adding to the water level of the river. He smiled when he thought about his bathroom oath. *Hold it till I explode. Yeah. Right.*

He zipped up his pants, then absentmindedly ran his thumbs down the red stripes. "Red stripes mean a Red Sox player has strong legs," he mumbled. *Strong legs to work in the fields. Strong legs so they won't starve.* He didn't know much about where he was, but he knew this family depended on him. He made a silent oath to help them in any way he could. And this one wouldn't be like the bathroom oath. He'd keep this one.

He looked up at the full moon and wondered if it was the same one he had seen at Jason's house the night before. *Couldn't be.* He remembered capturing the glow of the full moon in the dark glass the Wizard gave him. He reached into his back pocket and pulled out the glass. He wasn't looking for answers, just something familiar. The moon through Jason's pepper tree as his friends snored in the tent. Pizza. French toast. The Red Sox. His mom and dad. Heck, he'd even take his sister Marcia right now.

Checking the moon's position over his shoulder, he twisted the glass, making careful adjustments so the moon would be reflected right in the center. He felt his heart stop. Instead of the full moon, he saw the face of the Wizard.

Flattop had seen mini-televisions before, but this was pow-
ered by the warm glow of moonlight. Through some kind
of strange magic, Flattop Kincaid was watching the "Wizard
Show" on his own one-of-a-kind, dark glass TV. He steadied
the glass to the precise angle that kept the Wizard in full
view.

"Marvin, my boy! It's about time you looked in here."
The Wizard smiled mischievously and waved his fingers in
a tiny greeting.

"Where are you? Where am I?" Flattop questioned him
anxiously.

The Wizard raised his eyebrows. "Where do you think
you are?"

"I think I'm in my stupid game."

"Very good." The Wizard chuckled.

Flattop glared at the Wizard. "Yeah, well you wouldn't
think it was so funny if you were stuck here." He began a
list of complaints on his other hand. "They don't have bath-
rooms, they don't wash their dishes, they sleep on their
kitchen table—"

"It's 1150 A.D. This is the way people live."

"They eat this porridge stuff—" Flattop stopped in mid-sentence and looked back into the glass. "It's what?"

"1150 A.D." The Wizard grinned from ear to ear. "Welcome to the Middle Ages."

"Where's my mom and dad? What happened to my house?"

"Back in your century, safe and sound," the Wizard reassured him.

"What'll my mom do when she finds out I'm gone?"

"She hasn't noticed."

"Well, when she does, she's gonna have a cow." Flattop's voice grew louder as he got more frustrated with the Wizard's apparent lack of concern.

"Marvin—"

"And stop calling me Marvin."

"Very well . . . Flattop. You are indeed in the very game you bought from that handsome and charming fellow at the swap meet." The Wizard fluffed his long white beard and struck a pose in the dark glass.

Flattop rolled his eyes and heaved a sigh. It was very hard to be patient with an uncooperative wizard.

"You have been deposited, Red Sox uniform and all, somewhere in merry old England—to live as they lived."

Flattop pulled the glass closer to his face and stomped his foot. "But this is real! People die here! John and Ruth already lost a baby and a kid my age. They want me to take their son's place and work in the fields or they're probably going to starve to death."

"They're *serfs*, Flattop."

"Huh?"

The Wizard spoke in a softer, sympathetic tone, "Serfs. Peasants. That's what their life is like."

"They think I'm rich or something, just because of this stupid uniform."

The Wizard winked and raised his hand to his mouth as

if he were sharing a secret. "That uniform is the best thing about your adventure. In this century, red satin is a highly prized material. Everyone will be convinced you are from a very wealthy family. That jacket alone will get you treated very well."

"Yeah," Flattop agreed. "John and Ruth think I'm from a noble family because of this jacket. I don't know if they would've helped me if they thought I was poor."

"Precisely, my boy." The Wizard winked. "But the rest of the uniform is a stroke of good fortune, too. You look so different that everyone will take for granted that you're not from this region. When you use those strange words like *yeah* and *cool*, the good people of the Middle Ages won't think twice about it." The Wizard's face got very solemn. "But watch that you do not dazzle them with knowledge from your century," he warned, "unless you want to be tortured for practicing witchcraft."

Flattop felt a little sick to his stomach. "Yeah, but if this is just a game . . ."

"When you play a computer game and someone gets killed, to you, he just disappears. But for the character inside the game, the reality is, he dies."

"Wait a minute!" Flattop stared into the glass. "You mean I could get killed?"

The Wizard nodded. "Yes, my boy, if you're not careful."

Panic clutched at Flattop's insides. "Then get me out of here! Let me go home."

"Aha!" The Wizard raised one crooked finger. "Now we come to the object of the game. You can't go home until you catch me. You must find me and touch the dark glass to my hand."

"But I don't know where you are!"

The Wizard raised his eyebrows and the corners of his mouth turned up in a bemused smile. "It wouldn't be very challenging if I just gave you a map, now, would it?"

Flattop was stuck. "Okay, okay. I'll play your dumb game. But you have to tell me the truth." Flattop kicked the ground with his baseball cleats and stammered through the next question. "My mom . . . she really doesn't miss me?"

The Wizard's face softened. "My boy, what kind of a game would this be if all the while you knew your parents were sick with worry about their young son? You must trust me on this. They will know nothing of your disappearance."

Flattop studied the Wizard's face in the glass. The guy looked sincere, all right. There was nothing to do but play the game and get home as soon as he could.

"How am I supposed to find you?"

"Keep your eyes open. You'll see me."

An owl's loud *whooooo* rang out from the distant forest, startling Flattop and sending a cold chill up his spine. He rubbed the goosebumps on his neck and looked toward the direction of the sound. When he looked back into the glass, the Wizard was gone. He captured the moon's reflection again, but the Wizard didn't reappear.

*So this is how we play the game,* he thought to himself. *I have to eat old porridge from dirty bowls and sleep on a tabletop with a family of five.* Mr. Hartman, his baseball coach, always said Flattop had lots of competitive spirit. That spirit was going to get him through this game a winner. "You'll see, Wizard," he said into the empty glass. "You'll see who wins."

Flattop shoved the glass into his back pocket and headed back to the hut. He began to form a strategy to win this game and not get killed in the process. He'd seen time machine shows on television. The one thing that time travelers always did was go along with everything—try not to stick out. Granted, his baseball uniform didn't exactly blend in, but like the Wizard said, he could use that to his advantage.

He decided to stick with the story about robbers killing his rich, noble parents. But he'd cross his fingers when he said it so he wouldn't jinx his real mom and dad. Besides, everybody knows you can tell a whopper of a lie as long as you've got your fingers crossed. And he'd work hard to help John and Ruth until it was time to go home.

He slipped in through the doorway and quietly tiptoed across the dirt floor. He was thankful everyone was asleep so he didn't have to explain why he was gone so long.

He took off his jacket and gently pulled himself onto the mattress, wincing at every crackle and crunch of the straw inside. As he drew the big, heavy blanket over himself, he got another whiff of all those unwashed bodies underneath. But the satisfaction of having some questions answered made him feel peaceful inside, and he knew he'd fall sound asleep. Little George snuggled up next to him. For the first time in his life, Flattop felt like a big brother. He put a protective arm around George and closed his eyes.

When morning came, Flattop guessed he'd been sweating all night, because his uniform was damp. He wondered if maybe he caught the fever that John and Ruth talked about. But he felt fine. As he pulled back the blanket to get out of bed, his nose was struck with an unmistakable odor that he had smelled before.

Little George had wet the bed.

"Oh, no!" Flattop half-whispered as he rolled out of the bed. The sun wasn't up yet, so he couldn't see very well. He stood on the hard dirt floor and patted his uniform to find out how much of it was wet. "Oh, man. . . ." he complained as he sized up the areas of his shirt and pants.

"What is the trouble, son?" John's voice cut through the early morning stillness of the hut. Flattop heard the rustle of the straw mattress and looked up to see the shadowy figures of the whole family sitting up, watching him.

"George wet the bed."

"Is that all?" John chuckled. "He does that almost every night."

Ruth added, "He is still young, Flattop."

"Yeah, but I'm all wet."

Catherine giggled. "It will dry."

"The weather is warmer now," Margaret said. "You will be dry as soon as the sun is out."

"But it stinks!" Flattop argued.

"The smell will go away when it dries," Ruth assured him.

"It has happened to each of us many times and you do

not notice it on our clothes, do you?" John asked. With what little light there was, Flattop could see John holding out part of his tunic, inviting Flattop to take a test sniff.

"No, I believe you," Flattop said quickly. "It's just that . . ." Flattop's creative mind kicked into gear. "I only have one of these uniforms, and it's all I've got left to remember my family."

Ruth grabbed her husband's arm and whispered, "John!"

"You remember your family then?" John asked cautiously.

"Well, I remember everything until the robbers attacked us." Flattop crossed his fingers.

"I knew it!" John looked at Ruth. "It was the Robber King."

"Yeah, that's who it was. Anyway, now I'm all alone." Seeing this as a perfect opportunity to let them know they weren't taking unnecessary risks by keeping him, he added, "No one is going to be looking for me or thinking that I'm stolen or anything."

John looked at Ruth and touched her hand. "You see?" he said softly to her. "Nothing to worry about." Ruth smiled and nodded.

Just then the pigs joined the conversation with their snorts and grunts, and the chickens flapped down onto the floor, clucking and pecking.

"We have wasted enough time today," John announced. "Up and about, everyone."

While Flattop stood in the middle of the hut in his wet uniform, the family got out of bed, moved the mattress, opened the door and chased the chickens and pigs outside. He remembered his strategy to go along with everything, but he really needed to wash his uniform. Seeing John lifting the lid to another wooden chest in a corner of the room, he went to plead his case. "I know you don't think this is a big deal, but if this uniform gets stained—"

"Here, lad." John handed him a heavy woolen tunic and a pair of moth-eaten leggings. "These should do."

Flattop took the clothes. "Thanks. I'll give them back as soon as I wash my stuff."

"There is no hurry, lad." John closed the lid to the trunk. "They belonged to my son. I am saving them for Little George now."

"Don't worry," Flattop assured him. "I won't wreck them or anything."

John put his hand on Flattop's shoulder and looked steadily into his eyes. "I welcome you into my family, Flattop."

"Thanks." Flattop looked around for a place to change his clothes, then remembered there were no other rooms. He could either change inside the house in front of Ruth and the girls or outside in front of—well—whoever was out there. He walked to the corner where the pigs had slept because that looked the darkest.

He pulled off his uniform shirt and red-sleeved T-shirt underneath. He quickly grabbed the rough, scratchy tunic and threw it over his head. It seemed a little small, but he didn't care. He slipped his uniform pants off and pulled the leggings on underneath the tunic.

Except for his baseball cleats and his haircut, he looked like the rest of John and Ruth's family now. Their son's clothes were a pretty good fit. Flattop allowed himself a moment to really think about that, then he decided not to do it again. It was too eerie to think about wearing a dead kid's clothes.

Flattop saw Ruth stir the embers from last night's fire, then add more wood. Breakfast would be ready soon. He grabbed his uniform and took off running toward the river. When he got to the water's edge, he saw people on both sides, rinsing out clothes, tossing garbage or going to the bathroom in the same water. Now he knew why Ruth wouldn't let him drink it. He looked at the yellow stains on his uniform pants, then at the water.

Though he wondered how clean his uniform was going to get, he also realized this was his best shot. He let the water run through the two shirts and the pair of pants, scrubbing the material against a domed rock, like he had seen in a National Geographic special. The water temperature was like the ocean in winter, which was usually around fifty-five degrees. When his hands were too cold to stay in the water any longer, he wrung out the shirts and pants and headed back to the house.

That's when he saw the wagon. It sat abandoned on the edge of the forest. Flattop hadn't been in the Middle Ages long, but he knew that wagon hadn't been there yesterday, so he investigated. As he got closer, curiosity was replaced by shock as he realized there were bodies slumped over the side.

He looked back at the hut, wondering if he should yell for help. Then he realized that if John and Ruth didn't understand about washing dishes to kill germs, they probably didn't know anything about first aid, either. He shuddered as he remembered the medicine Ruth gave him last night. No doubt the people in the wagon needed more care than that.

He took off on a dead run to help. *First aid*, he thought to himself. *Bandages. Paramedics. 911.* Was there *anything* he could do? *Gotta help.* He was about thirty yards from the wagon when he saw all the blood. Warning bells went off in his head and he knew he should turn and run away, but he felt himself being drawn closer.

For an instant, he felt like the star of a TV murder mystery who discovers a crime, then solves it all by himself. But this was no television show, and the reality of death sickened him. A man was slumped across the driver's seat with an arrow through his back. His eyes were open and a trickle of blood had dried at the corner of his mouth.

Flattop walked around to the far side of the wagon. Two women and a boy about Flattop's age lay draped over the side in a bloodied mess of stab wounds and slit throats. He put his hand to his mouth to fight the sudden urge to throw up. His eyes filled with tears as he studied the look of frozen terror on the face of the dead boy. He wondered what it must have felt like to have a knife plunged in his heart or dragged ear to ear across his throat.

Flattop started to sweat and had trouble catching his breath. "Who would do this?" he asked himself in a half-whisper. He turned his back on the dead bodies and concentrated on taking slow, deep breaths until his head stopped pounding and the world stopped spinning.

At his feet lay three open trunks, their contents thrown all over the ground. It looked like robbery. Fear clutched at Flattop's heart. *The Robber King.* The thief John and Ruth talked about. The man they believed killed Flattop's parents. Flattop backed away from the wagon and stumbled on something that made a hollow *clunk* in the dirt. A gold cup with red jewels stuck to the sides. *The Robber King must've dropped it when he got away,* Flattop thought, as he pictured a huge, monstrous man stomping off into the woods with a sack of loot in one hand and a blood-covered knife in the other.

Suddenly Flattop gasped. What if the Robber King was watching him right now? Fear made the hair on the back of his neck stand straight up. He hugged the wrinkled, wet mass of his baseball uniform tight against his borrowed tunic and ran to the hut without looking back.

He charged inside, startling the chickens by the door and sending them flying.

"Goodness, lad," John said. "What troubles you?"

Flattop paused for a second to catch his breath and slow

down his pounding heart. "There's a bunch of people killed out there!"

Ruth stopped stirring the porridge and looked at Flattop. "Killed?"

"Yeah." Flattop nodded. "Look!" He ran to the door, gesturing wildly.

John walked to the door and focused on the wagon in the distance.

"I think it was the Robber King," Flattop said. "Their throats are cut, just like you said."

John nodded in silent agreement. "He is the devil's beast." While they watched, six men on horseback galloped up to the murder scene and dismounted.

"Lord Hemstead's men have arrived," John said, sighing. "Now we can lay this matter to rest."

"But what about all those dead people?" Flattop asked.

John glared at him. "What would you have us do? Say we saw the bodies? They would charge *us* with the robbery."

"No, they wouldn't," Flattop argued.

"If we were found anywhere near the wagon, we would be put to death as thieves."

"But the Robber King—"

"We are serfs, Flattop," John reminded him.

Flattop thought about his own century and all the juries, judges and lawyers who helped people get a fair trial. Apparently, being poor was crime enough in the Middle Ages.

"I just want to help," Flattop muttered.

"Then never again mention any of this."

Flattop looked around the hut to see John, Ruth, their son and daughters all staring at him. He sighed in defeat and uncrumpled the wet baseball uniform he'd been carrying. *I just want to help,* he thought, pouting to himself.

Having spread his wet clothes across the pig trough, he took his place at the breakfast table in time for prayer. He felt a twinge of nausea and didn't know if it was from the grisly sights at the murder scene or the porridge in his bowl that'd been sitting in the cauldron all night, only to be reheated for breakfast.

He remembered, too, that the bowls hadn't been washed. *Go along with everything. Try not to stick out.* Mustering all his courage, he lifted the bowl to his mouth and shoved the thick porridge in with his fingers, just like the rest of the family.

Surprisingly it wasn't bad, once he got past the germ thing. He thought of boiling a bucket of river water to teach them how to do dishes, but he wasn't sure you could boil that water enough to make it safe. Instead, he did what everyone else did. He used his hands to scrape the inside of the bowl as clean as possible.

When John finished the last fingerful of porridge from his bowl, he said, "The sun is almost up. We must leave for Lord Hemstead's fields." Flattop collected the bowls and, with a sigh of surrender to the serf's way of life, put them in the storage chest. Ruth pushed Margaret's hair away from her face and back into her dirty linen scarf, then changed her mind and untied the scarf. While Ruth sifted through a collection of small scraps of material, John watched Margaret practice her curtsy.

"We hope to place her in Lord Hemstead's castle," John explained. She would eat well, be cared for and it would mean one less mouth for us to feed."

"You want to give her away?" Flattop asked.

"We want to find a place for her," John said, then shrugged. "She's a girl. What can we do?"

"But she's your daughter."

Ruth walked to Margaret with a scrap of yellow material that was the right size for a scarf. Margaret lifted her hair and her mother knotted the scarf at the back of her neck. Ruth added, "She stands a better chance of surviving if she is accepted at the castle."

"What'll she do?" Flattop asked.

"Anything they ask," John said. "Right, Margaret?"

"Yes, Father." Margaret smiled and curtsied obediently.

"If she is taken in, we may be able to send Catherine there, too." Ruth fussed with the hem of Margaret's tunic.

John put on his hat. "Come. We must not be late." His family scurried out the door after him and began walking toward the hill in back of the hut.

Flattop trotted to the front of the group to walk alongside John. "Where are we going?"

"To Lord Hemstead's fields. Each family must give some of their labor to the tending of his crops," John answered.

"Can't he do his own farming?" Flattop asked.

John stopped dead and glared at Flattop. "Never say that in the presence of Lord Hemstead or his men. He gives us protection from thieves and scraps from his cookhouse. We have worked hard to remain in his favor."

"Sorry." Flattop felt his face turn bright red. "I didn't mean to say anything wrong."

John turned his gaze toward the top of the hill and started walking again. "It is best to say nothing, son. You will live longer if you do not call attention to yourself."

Flattop thought everybody wanted attention. Back home, there were celebrities in every walk of life, all trying to get attention. There were magazine covers featuring motocross riders, surfers, skateboarders and software designers. Even his sister, Marcia, wanted to be a supermodel. "Do you think my eyes should be bluer?" she'd ask as she stared into the full-length mirror for hours. "I can get colored contacts."

Flattop sighed, then watched Ruth pushing at Margaret with one hand and pulling Catherine and George up the hill with the other. Eye color was the least of their worries. Staying alive was more important.

When they reached the top of the hill and looked out, Flattop saw Hemstead Castle for the first time.

Flattop stood at the top of the hill watching serfs gather at the drawbridge below. He had seen "Sleeping Beauty's Castle" at Disneyland and assumed that all castles had straight rows of perfectly-cut gray brick and arched windows with stained glass. But this place was a slapped-together mixture of odd shaped rocks and wood with no real windows at all.

"Come," John said. "Let us fetch our seed and tools."

With that, the whole family jogged down the hill toward the drawbridge, with Flattop following. He felt his baseball cleats sink deep into the wet dirt and grass. When he reached the bottom, he inspected them for caked-on mud. That's when he noticed that John's family had pieces of leather and cloth tied around their feet.

Catherine was busily pushing stray pieces of straw back inside her shoes. Flattop had a piece of rye grass in his high tops one time and it drove him crazy. He couldn't let Catherine go on like that "Wait. She's got straw in her shoes."

Ruth bent down to adjust Catherine's laces. "It keeps her feet warm." When she was finished, Ruth walked over to Margaret and tucked wisps of the girl's nut brown hair into the yellow scarf.

As Flattop watched, he felt a small hand glide into his and hang on. He looked to see Catherine smiling up at him like an adoring sister. He had never seen that look on his own sister's face. In fact, if he ever did anything like that to Marcia, she would roll her eyes upward, heave a dramatic sigh and say, "Would you just get away and let me live my life?"

Flattop decided not to be mean like that. Besides, it felt pretty good being the oldest for a change. He smiled, gave the six-year-old's hand a squeeze, and said, "Lead the way."

Catherine took off running and practically tore Flattop's arm right out of the socket. As he struggled to get his feet back under him and keep up with her pace, he could hear John and Ruth laughing together. It made him miss his own mom and dad. In that split second, he hoped the Wizard was right and his parents didn't know he was gone.

As they got closer to the castle, Flattop could see little narrow slits at the top of the castle wall. At the base, the heavy wooden drawbridge extended out over a moat. He slowed down, then tugged on Catherine's arm so another man and woman could walk in front of them onto the drawbridge.

Flattop remembered the moat at Disneyland, where white swans glided around statues and flowers. But this moat stunk. It smelled like that time Pizza World had the sewer problem and no one wanted to eat there for a whole week. He took a quick look into the stagnant water covered with a brownish, rotting foam. And people said pollution was bad in *his* century.

Waiting for the rest of the family to catch up, Flattop got a closer look at the serfs entering the castle. He also saw a steady stream of women and children leaving with rakes, shovels and pick axes, while the men toted big cloth bags full of seed. He stood by, ready with a polite smile for anyone who looked at him. But no one did. Hunched over, eyes focused on the ground, they never looked up—not even at the guard on the drawbridge.

Flattop heard a sound like distant thunder coming from inside the castle walls. Catherine gripped his hand and stepped back. The noise got louder. Flattop pried his hand from Catherine's and walked onto the drawbridge. A man riding a huge white horse burst out of the tunnel and galloped toward him.

As the horse approached, Flattop saw the rider's tunic, a bright red lion on a yellow background. He also heard Catherine shout, "Flattop! Stand aside!"

Next, he saw the glint of a metal helmet, which looked like an upside-down bowl, and the polished steel of a sword that hung at the rider's waist and clattered against his stirrups.

Two chickens squawked and flew from the drawbridge. A young child screamed in fright.

Then Flattop saw the hawk, reddish brown with a leather hood covering its head, perched regally on the rider's forearm. Flattop knew he would always remember that . . . and the angry, "Out of my way, varlet!" the rider shouted as he knocked him to the side of the drawbridge.

Flattop managed to cling to the huge chains which attached the bridge to the castle, or he would've been swimming in the moat. *Watch where you're going, you stupid creep!* That's what Flattop thought of saying. But then he remembered the sword.

He turned to watch the rider gallop away, and saw that a second figure on horseback had been following closely behind. He was smaller and wore a gray hood. He also had a hawk on his arm. The first rider never turned around to see if Flattop was all right. The gray-hooded one did.

John and Ruth rushed to Flattop. "There, lad," Ruth said as she felt his shoulder. "Was it here that he hit you?"

Flattop winced. "Yeah. Stupid jerk."

"Quiet, son," John whispered. "He is Sir Humphrey, the bravest knight in the land."

"Yeah? Well he's the stupidest one, too," Flattop grumbled.

"His father is the lord who owns these lands," John added.

Flattop rolled his shoulder around, then rubbed it. "So that gives him the right to smack little kids around?"

"Come, lad." John grabbed Flattop's good arm. "He is a very powerful knight. He could have killed you today and no one would think any less of him. Be grateful that he saw fit to spare your life."

Flattop rubbed his shoulder. It hurt. But he could've been killed. The Wizard wasn't joking around. This game was for keeps.

John and his family talked to the guard on the drawbridge. Flattop heard John explain that Flattop was the recently orphaned child of his sister. The guard bought it. He motioned for them to enter the castle.

They all huddled together as they scurried across the drawbridge. Flattop glanced quickly at the moat and winced at the thought of almost landing in the stinking muck. They walked past the big, open door made of iron and wood and stepped into the short, dark tunnel.

Flattop ran his fingers over the rough stone walls. They were grimy and cold, and the slime in the cracks made him shudder.

He looked up to see a huge iron gate hanging overhead.

"Hey!" he blurted out. "That's the gate that slams down to keep the enemy out during an attack!" He struck a pose with one fist in the air. "Yes! I recognized something!" But that victorious feeling vanished when he saw John's entire family looking at him curiously.

*Uh-oh. They think I'm acting weird again.* Flattop looked around the tunnel, then finally said, "It's just that we don't really have those gates where I come from."

"By what means do you protect your castles in California?" John asked.

Flattop scrunched the rough fabric of his tunic with his left hand while he mentally fished for answers. "Well, we have dead bolts and burglar alarms." Flattop knew he was in over his head. "And cops," he added. One more quick look at their puzzled faces and he knew he'd never be able to explain this stuff without sounding crazy, so he shrugged his shoulders, pointed up to the gate and forced a weak chuckle. "Come to think of it, we have something just like this."

John and Ruth looked at each other, then at Flattop. Little George stared at Flattop then grabbed his mother's tunic and leaned into her leg. Flattop scolded himself for opening his big, fat mouth in the first place.

"Well," John said. "Let us fetch the seed."

They emerged from the tunnel into a bustling alley full of people and animals. A serf led a cow through the narrow walkway. A cat and her five kittens followed. A flock of sheep was herded out through the tunnel by two shepherds.

"Where are they going?" Flattop asked.

"To pasture," John replied.

A rooster strutted back and forth in front of the hen house as though he were on patrol. Two girls about Flattop's age skipped past him with baskets full of rich, dark blackberries. The ripe berries left a scented trail that made Flattop hungry for a peanut butter and jelly sandwich. The sounds of people and animals were punctuated by the hammering of a sweaty blacksmith as he shaped red-hot iron into a wheel rim for a broken cart.

Flattop's nose was filled with the heavenly aroma of cooking food. After two meals of porridge served in dirty bowls, it was comforting to know that *someone* was eating well. Ruth and Margaret walked down the alley as it curved to the right and headed toward the food smells. The aroma of roasting ham hypnotized Flattop, so he tagged along.

They came to the open door of a busy kitchen. Though it was early morning, fires blazed in a huge roasting pit and in the hearth. Fifteen men and women chopped, sliced, mixed and basted meats, vegetables and fruits. Over the pit, an entire pig was fastened to a pole, and two muscular men slowly turned it over the flame. Drops of juice sizzled as they hit the iron grill below, then fell into the flames. The edges of the grill were lined with juicy racks of ribs, being checked and turned by a another kitchen helper. Flattop crossed his arms over his stomach, hoping to quiet the ferocious growling inside.

Ruth glanced over her shoulder and saw him standing behind her. "Boy, why have you followed?"

Flattop couldn't open his mouth. It was watering so much he was afraid he'd drool all over his chin. He took a couple of quick swallows, then shrugged his shoulders.

"Stand back." Ruth gestured for him to move away from the door. "This is Margaret's only chance."

Flattop shuffled to one side and stayed out of sight, happy to breathe in the aroma of barbecuing meat.

"What is it, then?" a grouchy female voice asked from within the kitchen.

"The girl," replied Ruth, shoving Margaret in front of her. "Can you use her today in the cookhouse?"

"We have all the help we need," came the reply.

"She is a good worker. Sturdy. She can help you cook or clean or serve."

"Not today."

"Later then? Perhaps she can be of help later?"

"Bring her by and we shall see. Good day." The voice faded back into the hiss of cooking meat and the clang of iron pots.

"Later then, yes. Thank you, good mistress," Ruth called after the woman. Then, grabbing Margaret by the shoulders and pushing the girl ahead of her, she hurried back toward the castle entrance. Flattop quietly fell in step beside them.

"Who was that?" Flattop asked.

"Lady Hemstead," Ruth said in a half whisper. "It is she who decides which children shall be chosen to work in the cookhouse. Margaret has a very good chance." Ruth tugged at the left sleeve of Margaret's tunic to make it even with the right one.

Flattop glanced over his shoulder. "She didn't sound too friendly. Are you sure you want Margaret to work there?"

Ruth stopped suddenly and turned to face Flattop. "See here, lad. I know what is best for my child. If Margaret is to have a chance at a better life, it will be through the good graces of the lady of the castle." Ruth took a step closer and wagged her finger at him. "I will not have you ruin it with your thoughtless judgments."

Margaret wrapped her arms around Ruth's waist and cuddled against her mother. Ruth's anger stopped as quickly as it started. She smoothed her tunic, pulled a stray piece of hair away from her face and headed toward the drawbridge.

Flattop's heart pounded as he watched her walk away from him. "Wait a minute!" he shouted. "Wait!" He ran to catch up with her. "Look, I just meant—Margaret deserves better than just working in a—a cookhouse all her life."

Ruth slowed her pace.

"She's a really nice girl and I just thought maybe she could go to school or something."

Ruth stopped and turned around. "Flattop, I do not know how you do things in California, but here, the lady of the castle will teach her many things. Medicinals, herbs, cooking, running a household—"

"I might even learn to read," Margaret chimed in.

Ruth's voice became soft. "She will be fed and clothed and well cared for. She will grow to outlive us all."

Flattop could see in Ruth's eyes the same concern he often saw in his mother's. Whether she was bugging him about his college plans or trying to get him to eat vegetables, he always saw that glimmer of his mom's love somewhere deep in her eyes. Margaret was lucky to have a mom who loved her enough to want to give her up. Margaret was lucky to have a mom.

Flattop stepped up and looked into Ruth's face. "Sometimes I say really stupid stuff." Flattop felt his eyes flood with tears. He stared at the ground and swallowed hard to keep his voice from catching. After what seemed like an hour, he added, "Please don't be mad at me. I don't have anybody. . . ."

He couldn't bear to look at her again. Suddenly, he felt her arms wrap around him. "My lad, you have come to us with your strange words and your strange ways and sometimes I do not know what to think. But do not fear. You are not alone."

She held him close, and in the safety of that hug, with people bustling all about them, Flattop mumbled, "I'm sorry."

Ruth gave him an extra squeeze and whispered, "So am I, lad. So am I."

It felt good to be hugged by a mom. Anybody's mom.

Ruth patted him on the back. "Well now, let us find John. There is much work to do." She led Flattop and Margaret back to the entrance. Margaret held Flattop's hand as the two of them followed Ruth through the busy alley.

They walked past a bakery where a fat old man not only baked bread, but ground the wheat to make it. The warm, yeasty smells coming from the clay oven made Flattop's mouth water again. At this rate, he guessed he'd run out of spit before the day was over.

They sidestepped a barking dog that was being chased by two angry geese, rounded a corner, passed by the drawbridge and followed the alley's second curve. Flattop looked into a stable to see several big horses like the one the pushy knight was riding. They passed separate barns for cows and pigs, where animals rested on mounds of straw, just like they did at the Junior Farmers Exhibit at the County Fair.

"Ho, there!"

Flattop looked up to see John walking toward them, followed by Catherine and Little George. John carried a large burlap sack of seed over his left shoulder and cradled two shovels and a pick axe in his right arm. Ruth hurried to him and took the rakes, handing one to Flattop. They all walked back to the drawbridge and out onto the vast stretch of unplowed land that lay not far from the castle.

Margaret, Catherine and George ran ahead, giggling and laughing. Ruth excitedly told John that Margaret might get to work in the cookhouse later in the day. While they talked about Margaret's future, Flattop lagged behind. Carrying his axe over his shoulder like a rifle, he gazed out at the scenery. That's when he saw them—the pushy knight and his little gray-hooded companion.

They were riding hard and fast about two hundred yards straight ahead, right where John and Ruth's three children were walking. An unexplainable protective streak made Flattop run past the adults to be with the three young kids, just in case they needed him. After all, he had dealt with this bully once today.

By the time Flattop reached the kids, the knight and his partner had ridden on. They all watched as the knight released his hawk. The bird soared upwards, then dove straight to the ground, striking at something. With a whistle from the knight, the hawk returned to his arm.

The knight's friend then released his hawk. It shot straight up into the air, then took off for the distant forest. The knight and his friend galloped after the wayward bird, whistling, waving their arms and shouting.

The whole scene did Flattop a lot of good to know that those two road hogs couldn't get any respect from a stupid bird. *Why don't you try knocking him into the stupid moat?* Flattop snickered to himself as he watched the two men disappear into the woods.

When they got to their section of Lord Hemstead's field, the hard work began. Everybody, including Little George, had a job to do. Flattop and Ruth used shovels to dig furrows in the cold, wet ground. Sometimes the earth was packed so hard that John had to use an axe to chop up the thick, brownish-black clods. Margaret and Catherine used pointed sticks to gouge deep, straight lines into the soil. George crawled on his hands and knees, squashing the dirt clods and carefully placing seed into the little furrows.

Flattop half-expected the kids to lose interest and start goofing around. If he and his friend Jason were their age, they'd be running around and having fake sword fights with the sticks. Once, he and Jason got into a mud-throwing fight while they were weeding Mrs. Lawson's garden. They had to hear a little yelling from their moms, and it took the boys forever to wash all the dirt out of their hair, but it was no big deal. Maybe Margaret, Catherine and Little George knew their lives depended on hard work.

Flattop stuck his shovel into the heavy clods again. Even though it was cold, he was working up a good sweat. He could feel a moustache of perspiration growing above his lip. He turned his head toward the rough woolen sleeve of his tunic and wiped his face. There was that smoky, sweaty scent. He smelled just like the rest of them now.

Flattop looked around and saw other families hard at work in the fields. No one talked. The only sounds were the thud of the iron pick axe as they chopped into the ground and an occasional "oomph" from Ruth as she pushed her shovel into the stubborn soil.

Flattop thought about singing a song to help the time go by, but he could only think of those stupid Beatles songs his mom and dad sang in the car. That and "Ninety-nine Bottles of Beer on the Wall." So he just kept shoveling. A couple of times they heard the high-pitched screech of a hawk, and everyone glanced toward the forest. Flattop smiled as he thought of the pushy knight and his buddy chasing the runaway bird.

Just as they finished their third row of seeding, Catherine cried out, "Crows!" More than a dozen, to be exact. They were pecking at the burlap seed bag, looking for lunch. Margaret and Catherine ran for the bag. They tore the scarves off their heads and frantically waved them, scattering the big black birds in every direction. But before the girls could celebrate their victory, the crows had swooped down into the freshly dug seed furrows.

"Get them, Flattop!" Margaret shouted.

Flattop lurched forward, tripped over his own shovel and fell face first in the moist, sticky earth. Not only did he feel like a klutz, he heard Little George laughing. He made a mental note to get that little kid later. He lifted his head out of the soil and saw the crows take off in a flurry of black feathers. He struggled to his knees and looked at his dirt-smeared tunic. *Stupid dumb birds!*

As he looked up, he saw a hawk, sly and strong, perched on the sack of seed. The rest of the family backed away. Flattop was so mad at the crows that right now he hated all

65

birds. He wiped his dirty hands on his tunic, slowly stood up and grabbed his shovel. Then he let out a yell and charged toward the hawk.

"Flattop! No!" shouted Ruth.

"The knight! The knight!" screamed Margaret.

"No, boy! Not the hawk!" shouted John.

Flattop thrust the shovel toward the bird, but the hawk was airborne in the blink of an eye. Frustrated, Flattop waved his shovel above his head, chasing after the hawk. That's when he noticed the knight and his friend riding toward him. He stopped in his tracks. The hawk came to rest on the forearm of the knight's companion, who quickly thrust a small leather hood over the bird's head.

The knight rode slowly up to Flattop. Flattop heard one of the girls take a quick, frightened gulp of air. He didn't have the nerve to look the knight in the face, so he stared at his baseball cleats. The horse hung its head over Flattop's and snorted. Flattop felt the warm, wet breath push through his hair and slide down his neck. He heard the metal-on-metal scrape of the knight's sword leaving its holder. No doubt about it, he was dead. He closed his eyes, waiting for the killing blow.

Instead, he felt the cold steel under his chin, tilting his face upward. He opened his eyes and gazed up at the sneering man in the bowl-shaped helmet and yellow-and-red tunic. The knight's leather-hooded hawk sat blindfolded and passive on his left arm. "Chasing the hawk our way?" he asked with a scornful smile.

Flattop ran through a quick list of possible replies. He finally came up with, "Huh?"

"Filthy varlet," the knight snarled as he put his sword away. Turning toward the castle, he spurred his horse and galloped away.

Flattop jumped to the side as the horse took off. He was

pretty shook up, but at least he was alive. That's when he realized the knight's companion was riding up to him.

For the first time, he got a look at the young man's face in the gray hood. His sister, Marcia, dated guys who looked like this. What was he—sixteen, maybe? *If he tries anything, I'll pull him right down off that horse,* Flattop thought to himself. *Big, tough bird man. I can take him.*

The young man nodded and said, "Thank you for your efforts to recover my hawk." Then he turned and galloped after the knight.

Flattop's mouth dropped open in amazement. *Thank you for your efforts? Thank you? Hey, this guy isn't so bad. Thank you.* Flattop quickly waved to the young man. "Don't mention it. No problem."

He turned toward the rest of the family, still waving his hand and smiling. John stepped forward and smacked him right on the side of his head. It wasn't that the blow was hard, but it was a surprise, and it knocked Flattop to the ground. He rubbed the area between his cheek and ear and looked up at John, frightened and confused.

"You fool!" John shouted. "He could have killed us all! Or put us in the dungeon for good!"

Flattop protested. "What'd I do?"

John stepped back, never taking his eyes off Flattop. He took off his hat and ran his fingers through his sweaty hair. "Ruth . . ."

"Yes, husband," she replied quickly.

"Take Margaret back to the cookhouse. See if they will use her."

"Yes, husband." Ruth grabbed Margaret's hand and scurried off to the castle.

"Children! Mind the seed. Keep the crows away."

"Yes, Father," Catherine and Little George answered in unison, and ran to guard the bag.

John walked to Flattop and stood over him. Flattop cow-ered a little, thinking he was in for some kind of beating. But John just stared at him for what seemed like hours. Then he looked away, cleared his throat and said, "I am afraid I must let you go, boy."

Flattop sat up, straight as a board. "What do you mean?"

"You continue to place my family in danger with your foolish deeds."

*Stupid, stupid!* his mind scolded. *Why do I always do such stupid things?* Flattop scrambled to his knees. "Look, I know that was dumb. I just got mad because of the birds and the mud and—"

"You must leave us."

"What about me helping you so you won't starve? I'm strong, remember? I'm a good worker."

John straightened up and looked at his children, who were dancing circles around the seed bag. "Starving is a chance I will take. If you continue to stay with us, we will all surely be put to death."

"I promise. I won't do it again. I'll shut up. I won't chase birds. I swear—" Flattop's voice caught in his throat and tumbled out with a sob. "Please! Please! I swear I'll be good." The sobs came faster now. All the confusion of these past two days took the form of tears and rolled down his dirty cheeks onto the cold, damp ground. He was begging to eat porridge out of dirty bowls, begging to smell of dirt and sweat. He had nothing else.

John stood motionless, watching the boy at his feet. Finally, he sighed and said, "Very well, son. I will give you one last chance." He put a reassuring hand on Flattop's shoulder. "But you must mind yourself."

Flattop took a couple of deep sobbing breaths, then rubbed his eyes with the back of his hand. It took a minute for the words to sink in. *He could stay.* He wiped his drippy nose on the sleeve of his tunic and looked up. "I'll mind myself. I promise."

"Well, then, up with you, boy." John took hold of Flattop's upper arm and pulled him to his feet. He surveyed the head-to-toe dirt on the boy and added, "You must try to stay out of the wet soil for the rest of the day, or you will catch a chill."

Flattop let go with a relieved laugh. "I'll try." He brushed at the sticky, black soil on his tunic and pants, but it just smeared into the wool.

"Let it dry, son," John said. "It will be good as new." He looked out over the morning's work and picked up a shovel. "Now we must finish covering this seed before the birds return."

Flattop grabbed the other shovel and they began to push the loose dirt into the furrows, burying the seed. The musty scent of wet dirt was so strong that it was almost hard to breathe. Flattop hadn't been around that smell since he'd helped his dad drag the Little League field after a heavy rain. The dads always had to level the infield before a game. They took a piece of thick wood, tied chains to it and dragged it over all the dirt, to smooth it out. *Hey! Why don't we drag this field?*

"John, I've got an idea!"

"Now, Flattop—"

"No, it's okay. It won't get us in trouble."

Flattop found a fairly straight fallen tree limb and put the flattest side on the ground across the seed row. Then he and John grabbed hold of the ends and dragged the limb, watching it push the dirt into the furrow. John looked at Flattop and smiled in approval.

When they were finishing the last row, they heard Ruth calling them, "John! They gave her food!"

Ruth was running up the hill, waving. Margaret stumbled along behind, holding one of her tunics up like a big fabric bowl. Catherine and George jumped up and down, cheering. John applauded and laughed the first hearty laugh Flattop had heard in two full days.

## 13

It wasn't really food. It was more like table scraps. The kind you give a dog when the meal is over and your three-year-old cousin didn't eat all his peas. Flattop's share of the castle food was an apple core, some pear and apple peelings and the tops of two carrots. Actually, it wasn't table scraps at all—it was garbage. But John's family ate contentedly, spitting out seeds and gnawing at the orange bits of carrot left on the carrot greens.

He'd heard of people eating out of garbage pails before, but he'd never known anyone who actually did it. And he certainly didn't think he'd ever be one of them. But hunger got the best of him and Flattop soon understood how the poor and the starving didn't have the luxury of being picky eaters. For all he knew, these few scraps of garbage could be the thing that kept John's family from starving this year.

Flattop tried an apple peel. It was bitter and tough to chew but there was also a hint of the sweet, juicy apple that had ended up on somebody's plate in the castle. His mouth began to water and he chewed faster, until there was no flavor left. He gratefully swallowed it and took another bite.

He nibbled at the edge of a carrot top. It was a good

change of taste from the sweetness of the apple. The pear peelings were tricky. They were sweeter than the apple peelings, but more delicate. They had to be chewed slowly, so they'd last a long time. Finally, he came to the apple core he had saved for dessert. The sweet pulp left on the core was a gold mine of flavor. Except for the stem and the seeds, he ate the whole thing.

"That was wonderful, Margaret," John said, wiping his mouth and shaking a few wayward pear seeds off his tunic.

Ruth smiled and gently ran her fingers through Margaret's hair. "I told you they liked her."

"They want me to come back when their meal is finished," Margaret said proudly.

John stood up, took a deep breath and, with a satisfied smile, said, "Well, then. Let us earn our keep."

The family got up and spent the rest of the afternoon digging and seeding, then using the tree limb to drag the field and cover the seeds. After a couple hours of work, the family saw the knight and his buddy gallop into the forest carrying bows and arrows. Flattop decided it would be best if he didn't stop to watch them.

John peered at the sky. "Our work is finished for today." Flattop peeked at his watch. Four o'clock. *Time flies when you almost get thrown out of a family.* John picked up the axe and the remaining seed and led the way to the castle. Ruth followed, holding George's hand while the two girls playfully held onto her tunic.

Flattop wrestled with the two heavy shovels until Margaret tapped his shoulder. "May I help?"

Flattop smiled and handed one to Margaret. He watched her skip off to walk with her father. If she were in school, she'd only be in second grade, like Angela who lived down the street. *She'd be a Brownie and come around twice a year selling cookies and calendars. But here she's got to work in a*

71

*kitchen and eat garbage.* "What a waste," he muttered to himself.

They were almost to the drawbridge when the knight and his companion came barreling through. Flattop turned his back so the knight wouldn't pick on him. He wondered if the younger one saw him as he galloped by. He wasn't going to risk looking. One more screwup and he was out of John's family. Of course, at the rate he was going, he'd mess up something sooner or later. He decided he'd sneak out that night when everyone else was asleep and talk to the Wizard. Then he'd know what to do.

Once inside the castle walls, Ruth and Margaret headed for the cookhouse, and John, Flattop and the two kids went to return the tools and seed. As John waited in line with the other farmers, Flattop wandered down the alley to a door that said MEWS. He wondered if *mews* meant news and that's where they printed the newspaper. Maybe it meant kittens. His curiosity got the best of him and he peeked inside.

To his surprise, he discovered that *mews* must mean "hawk house," because there had to be twenty of them in there. Big, beautiful birds with mottled feathers of black, brown and gray, regally sitting on wooden perches. He stood in the half-open doorway and stared.

That's when he saw it. The bird that had gotten him in trouble. *That* one was different. There was something . . . something about the eyes. That bird knew things the other birds didn't know. He got a sudden chill of recognition.

"Wizard! It's you, isn't it?" The hawk flitted to the front of its cage and stared intently at Flattop. "How can you change into a—I mean—where's your hat?" Just then a hand roughly grabbed his arm and yanked him back into the alley.

"Remember your promise," John warned, and released his grip on Flattop's arm. Flattop nodded and silently followed him out of the castle, with Catherine and George tagging along behind. Flattop's mind raced. *The Wizard. Of course!*

*Hawks don't just sit around on seed bags and stare at people, like that one had.*

Ruth and Margaret ran to meet them. Margaret was carrying something wrapped in her yellow head scarf. "Look! More!"

"They gave her more food!" Ruth cried.

"And I am to come back tomorrow," Margaret said proudly.

John wrapped a protective arm around his daughter. "Good girl." The family practically skipped all the way home. Even Flattop was excited. Sure it was garbage, but it was a nice addition to the boring old porridge. Besides, now that he knew the Wizard had been watching him all along, he felt pretty good.

When they got to the hut, Flattop raised the sleeve of his jacket and peeked at his watch. Four-thirty in the afternoon. John stoked the fire and Ruth stirred the cauldron of porridge. Outside, Flattop showed the kids how to catch a pop fly. Using a tree branch, he carefully batted old, hardened dirt clods into the air. Margaret, Catherine and Little George squealed with delight as they tried to catch them.

When Ruth called them in, they rounded up the chickens and pigs and herded them into the house. Flattop got the bowls out of the big wooden chest. John and Margaret pushed the boxes and stools to the table. The porridge was dished out and Flattop couldn't believe how good it smelled. They bowed their heads over the hot, steamy goo while John said grace. Then bowls went up to mouths, and fingers eagerly pushed the porridge in.

When George had finished licking the inside of his bowl, Margaret brought the castle food to the table. Ceremoniously, she unwrapped the scarf to reveal three pieces of thick, dry bread soaked in some sort of brown juice. They voiced their solemn *oohs* and *ahhs* in half-whispers, except for George, who jumped up and down and clapped his hands.

John broke the bread into six pieces and passed it out.

73

Everyone ate slowly, savoring each bite. Flattop bit into the soggy middle. *French dip,* he thought. He remembered eating a French dip sandwich once when his parents took him to their favorite coffee shop. He thought he was going to get some kind of French fries and dip, but instead he got a roast beef sandwich on beef-juice bread.

That's what this was, without the roast beef. Just beef-juice bread. But after the second bite, he couldn't stop his mouth from watering. It tasted heavenly. He slurped his way through the soggy, stale chunk, trying to make it last as long as possible.

Maybe he just didn't appreciate French dip sandwiches the first time he'd had them. Maybe he'd had his heart set on pizza and hadn't really given them a chance. One thing was for sure. When he got home, he'd have more French dip sandwiches.

When the family had finished, they enjoyed a satisfied silence in the twilight for a good minute or two. Then it was bedtime. The stools and benches were pushed away and the bowls were put back in the chest. Flattop helped John carry the mattress to the table. Then they all piled into bed, pulling the heavy blanket over them. Flattop noticed that the stench of unwashed bodies didn't bother him as much tonight. Maybe he was too tired to care.

When he woke up again, it was dark. His elbow itched. He checked his watch. Four-thirty in the morning. He scratched his head, then his behind. *Mosquitoes? Nah.* Scratching his ankle, he slid out of bed and put on his baseball cleats. He crossed the room to where his baseball uniform had been drying, found his pants and took out the dark glass. After checking to make sure the rest of the family was asleep, he quietly pushed the scrap of wood to the side and squeezed out.

First things first. He had to find a bush. There was still enough of the full moon shining to light his way. He found a good bathroom location and dug a hole, the way they taught him at Boy Scout camp. As he perched above his outdoor toilet, he recalled his bathroom oath and how quickly he had broken it. Then he remembered the really awful part. There was no toilet paper.

He reached around him and pulled up some grass—lots of grass. After a couple of half-hearted attempts, he figured out how to get the job done. Then, like a cat, he kicked the dirt over his primitive toilet. He had to admit that it wasn't as bad as he thought it would be. John had offered him a handful of straw yesterday. Next time, he'd remember the straw.

Scratching an itch on his stomach, he walked out into the open where he could easily capture the moon's glow in the dark glass. At first, he could've sworn he saw the face of the hawk reflected back at him, then the Wizard's face appeared.

"Well, Marvin, my boy, you've had a busy day."

Flattop didn't want small talk. "That hawk. It was you, wasn't it?"

"Hmmm?"

"The hawk that other guy had. The one in the gray hood."

The Wizard rolled his eyes up and to the side as if in deep thought. "You mean, the knight?"

"No." Flattop shook his head. "The other one."

"Oh! The squire! He's a knight-in-training. He rides with the knight, helps him get dressed . . . eh . . . what was your question?"

Flattop took a deep breath then looked out across the river. He needed a minute to gather all his patience. "The squire's hawk. You were the squire's hawk, weren't you?"

"Goodness, Marvin, such a question!" The Wizard began to laugh.

"It *was* you! I knew it! If I had just touched you today, I could've gone home."

"Not so fast, my boy. You must touch *me*, in human form. Not some silly, feathered creature. And you must use the dark glass." The Wizard leaned into the glass till his eyes and nose filled the entire surface. "As I recall, you left the glass in your britches, did you not?"

"I don't have any pockets in these clothes," Flattop protested, as he bent down to scratch his leg.

The Wizard raised an eyebrow. "I see you've got something else in those clothes."

"What?" Flattop looked down at the tunic and leggings that were covered with dirt.

"Lice, for one." The Wizard shook his head.

Flattop stopped scratching. "You mean like that fourth-grader got when she tried on hats at a garage sale?"

"Bingo. You've probably got a few fleas, as well."

Flattop was pacing now, looking down at his clothes, shaking them. "How'd I get them?"

"Oh, don't be silly, Marvin. It would be stranger if you *didn't* get them."

This new knowledge was making him itch even more. "How do I get rid of them?"

"Catch me. Then you can go home to the land of flea collars and bug sprays."

"Very funny."

"Until then, try a bracing dip in the river. That's what the locals do."

Flattop started to ask another question, but the Wizard's image faded away. In its place appeared the face of the squire's hawk. With a wink and a high-pitched screech, it, too, disappeared.

Flattop was beginning to hate these moonlight sessions. He walked back to the hut, scratching his shoulder, then his side. When he got to the doorway, he stopped to rub his back along the rough wood.

In bed, he watched it get lighter and lighter outside, as he got itchier and itchier. He checked his watch. Five-thirty. He scratched his armpit good and hard. After another half hour, he couldn't stand it any longer. If he hurried, he could take the Wizard's advice and jump in the river before everyone else was up. He jumped out of bed, grabbed his baseball uniform, jacket and cleats and headed for the water.

At first, he was going to peel his clothes off and skinny dip. Then he realized the bugs were in the clothes too. He dipped his hand in the water. Pretty cold, all right. But his back itched like crazy. There was only one thing to do. With clenched fists and gritted teeth, he leaped in.

In the next split second he forgot how to breathe. He needed air, but his throat and lungs wouldn't work. He crossed his arms and pressed them into his stomach. That pushed the breath out. In a raw gasp, he gulped for air. He couldn't stand it much longer. To make sure he had no bugs in his hair, he dipped his head underwater. Icy cold pierced his ears and froze his brain.

Flattop tried to crawl out of the water quickly, but the weight of his soggy wool clothing seemed to add a hundred pounds to his body. He finally pulled himself onto the river bank, cold and exhausted. He tugged off the old clothes and replaced them with his baseball uniform.

"R—r—red s—s—sleeves m—m—mean," he stammered as his teeth chattered and his body shivered, "a R—r—red S—s—s—s—sox—Aw, f—f—forget it." He quickly threw on the rest of his clothes before he froze to death.

He stepped into his cleats, but his hands were shaking too hard to tie the laces, so he put on his jacket and jogged in circles by the river, hoping to build up some body heat.

When he finally got his shoelaces tied, he heard the screech of a hawk in Lord Hemstead's forest. He looked up. A flash of purple disappeared behind a tree. *The Wizard!*

Flattop took off in a dead run for the woods. This was his chance to go home.

······

# 14

The Wizard was an old guy. Even if he could run fast, he couldn't keep it up for long. Flattop caught another glimpse of a purple robe swinging out from behind a tree farther into the forest. He poured on the speed. This was going to be a piece of cake. He reached the tree and looked behind it.

No Wizard.

Flattop knew the Wizard wouldn't give up easily, but he also knew why Coach Hartman made all the Red Sox players run laps before and after practice: to keep them in shape. *White makes my steps sure and true,* he chanted to himself. *A Red Sox player is fast of foot.*

Flattop heard the Wizard's high-pitched cackle behind a fallen log in a tiny clearing about a hundred feet away. He took off again, running faster this time. With a victorious leap, he jumped on top of the log and looked around.

No Wizard.

The surrounding trees blocked out the early morning light and gave the forest a spooky feel. The musty smell of rotting, moldy leaves filled his nose. His own heavy breathing seemed even louder in the dark stillness. For a half second, he thought about all those mad slasher movies he wished he'd never seen.

The far-off echo of the Wizard's laugh floated toward him from the deepest part of the woods, and he began running again. He could feel his baseball cleats punching through the leaves and mud, giving him good traction. He'd catch the Wizard and home would be only moments away.

*Corn dogs,* he thought. *When I get home, I'm gonna eat a million corn dogs.* His brain conjured up a plate piled high with corn dogs next to a giant bottle of ketchup. *Corn dogs . . . and a shower,* he added. His mother would probably faint, but she didn't know what he'd been through in the last couple of days.

Flattop caught the faint smell of smoke and looked around for the source. Pale, ghostlike puffs were rising behind a clump of bushes about thirty yards away. He had found the Wizard's camp. Still on a dead run, Flattop reached into his hip pocket and pulled out the purple glass, ready to shove it into the Wizard's hand.

He blasted through a thin spot in the bushes, held the dark glass above his head, and shouted out a triumphant, "Yes!"

That's when Flattop discovered he was standing in front of three men, who looked very surprised and very sinister. In the stunned silence that followed, Flattop's gaze darted back and forth as he tried to size up the situation. He would've turned around and run away, but his legs had stopped working. So had his arms. He was still in that silly pose with one hand over his head.

That's when the weird-looking guy in the middle walked toward Flattop. He was dirty and fat, with thick eyebrows that formed a hairy ledge over his eyes and brown hair that seemed to tangle into his bushy, full beard. On his head he wore a gold-colored crown that looked like a bad metal-shop project. Several layers of metal chains and jeweled necklaces were fastened around his neck, and hung down the front of his ripped-up tunic. A black cape was attached to his shoulders by two jeweled pins. As he walked he flung the cape around, looking very dramatic.

Flattop saw the jewel-handled knife the man carried in his belt, as well as the thick wooden club that looked kind of like a baseball bat. Flattop slowly lowered his hand and stood at attention as the man approached him.

"We got us a visitor, men," he said. His breath smelled like rotten onions and spilled beer.

"Aye, my lord," one of the men replied.

Flattop felt his mouth drop open. *Lord?* Could this be Lord Hemstead, the guy who owned the castle, the land, the pushy knight and John's entire family?

The man circled slowly around Flattop. "Don't you know the meaning of private property, lad?"

Flattop felt his stomach drop to his knees. What had he done? He was so eager to catch the Wizard, he didn't realize he was trespassing in Lord Hemstead's forest. John said he could get killed for that.

"Speak up, boy!" the man shouted.

Flattop moved his mouth but no words came out. He was still thinking. He couldn't say he was going home to another century and he couldn't say he was chasing an enchanted wizard. They'd lock him up for sure. Or worse.

That's when he remembered John's story. He crossed his fingers in preparation, then he sniffled a little and did his best to look pathetic. "Please, sir. I am an orphan. My mother and father were killed last night."

"Last night?" the man asked. He squinted in order to study Flattop more closely. "How did it happen?"

Flattop sighed. He was never very good at lying, but this was life or death. "We were traveling. On vacation. We got a flat tire and—"

"A what?"

Flattop revised his story. "Our horse got sick. He was throwing up all over the place."

The man tilted his head to one side, the way a dog does when it doesn't understand something. "Strange," he said. "Horses do not . . . throw up."

"They don't? Well, that's not important." Flattop nervously adjusted his baseball cap, pulling it lower over his eyes. "What *is* important is that we were running late. We were driving through here at night and—"

"Through *here?*"

"No! I mean, not here, exactly. We were on the outside of the woods because we knew this was private property." Flattop waved his hands around for emphasis. "My dad said we shouldn't go in, even though my mom thought we could and—"

The man rubbed his dirty hand over his face and sighed. "How did you lose your parents, lad?"

"Well," Flattop paused to muster all the dramatic intensity he could. "We were robbed."

The man looked up, wide-eyed. "Robbed? You were robbed?" He looked at his companions then back at Flattop. "Tell me more, lad."

Flattop was pleased to see that the lie was going over so well. "I don't remember much. I got hit over the head, my mom and dad got killed and we got robbed."

The three men shook their heads and traded confused looks. That's when Flattop added, "And I know who did it."

The man clamped his strong hands on Flattop's shoulders and looked intently into Flattop's eyes. "Who was it, boy?"

Flattop held his head high and stared straight into the man's eyes. "It was the Robber King."

"The Rob—" The man's eyes widened in surprise as he took a step back.

Flattop nodded boldly—until he saw the man burst into laughter, joined by his two companions. "The Robber King, you say!" The man doubled over in hysteria. His companions slapped each other on the back as they gasped for breath between laughing fits.

After a couple of minutes, Flattop was downright disgusted with the way they were *still* laughing at his heartbreaking robbery story. Lord Hemstead hated the Robber King. Why would he find Flattop's story so funny?

Unless he wasn't Lord Hemstead.

*Serves me right for lying,* Flattop thought. The man he thought was Lord Hemstead was really the Robber King. The thief inspected Flattop's baseball hat and handed it to one of his buddies. Then he ran his hand along the shiny red satin sleeve of Flattop's baseball jacket.

" 'Tis a fine hand," he observed.

"It's a sleeve," Flattop corrected.

"I mean, 'tis nice cloth."

Flattop nodded. "Expensive, too."

"I will have it."

Flattop jerked his arms away from the Robber King. "No way." But before he knew it, he was staring at the pointed end of a nasty looking knife. "Oh, all right," he grumbled, angrily tugging the jacket cuff over his left hand.

It wasn't until he had trouble getting his right hand through the cuff that he realized he was still holding the dark glass. When he reached around to put it in his hip pocket, he felt the Robber King's knife poke his forearm.

"What is that?" He prodded Flattop's forearm until the dark glass was held up for everyone to see.

Flattop tried to remain calm on the outside, even though

alarm bells were going off all over his insides. He looked at the glass, then shrugged. "This? It's nothing. I found it in the dirt."

"I will have it, then."

"It's just a stupid piece of glass," Flattop snapped.

"Then you will not miss it."

Inside Flattop was screaming, *No! You can't have it! It's mine!* To his amazement, he discovered he was also screaming on the outside.

The Robber King grabbed Flattop's baseball shirt with one hand and held the knife to his neck with the other. "When I say something is mine, it is mine," he snarled. "Now, give me the glass."

Flattop handed the glass to the Robber King. It wasn't until the villain released him that Flattop realized he hadn't been breathing. He took a long gasp of air.

"Give me the overgarment, too."

His prized red satin baseball jacket slipped off his drooping, defeated shoulders. He loved that jacket, but his heart had broken when he'd given up the dark glass. It had been his only hope of going home, of seeing his mom and dad and even his stupid sister again. He felt hollow inside—hollow and hopeless.

He watched as the Robber King held the glass up and tried to look through it. He wanted to ask for it again, but decided that would just make it seem more valuable. He cringed as the Robber King spit on the glass, then rubbed it with his filthy hand. That's when he noticed new feelings building up inside him. Anger. Hatred. Rage. He discovered how brave someone could get when he has nothing to lose. He would get that glass back or die trying, because he, Flattop Kincaid, refused to be stuck in the porridge-eating, lice-infested Middle Ages forever.

Flattop watched as his one and only ticket home was passed from man to man for closer inspection. When it was returned to the Robber King, he stuck it inside Flattop's baseball hat and set it under a tree. Flattop's heart raced. As long as the glass was in plain sight, it would be easier to grab when the moment was right.

The Robber King tried on the satin baseball jacket. Even though it was an oversized jacket for Flattop, it was about twenty sizes too small for the Robber King. And he looked ridiculous with his black cloak sticking out from underneath.

But the Robber King didn't seem to mind. He rubbed his hands on the satin sleeves and smiled. After he was done modeling his new possession, he let his buddies try it on. One of the guys walked over to touch the red sleeves on Flattop's baseball T-shirt. The Wizard was right, red was a real attention-getter. All three outlaws ran their dirty fingers over the glossy red *RED SOX* that was sewn across the chest of his baseball shirt.

Flattop played it cool and kept his eye on the hat that held the dark glass. He would wait for the right moment to get his glass back. A horse's whinny brought him out of his thoughts. He looked around, hoping for a rescuer.

"My steed wishes some grain," the Robber King announced to his companions.

Flattop was delighted to hear there was a horse available. He might need it for a fast getaway once he took back the dark glass. Of course, the only riding he'd ever done was a pony ride or two when he was little, but he had watched a rodeo once. That should count for something.

The outlaws walked over to a rumpled pile of blankets and supplies and pulled out a brown sack that looked like the seed bag John's family had used the day before; but instead of seeds, the bag was filled with oats. Flattop figured he ought to have a look at the Robber King's horse before he needed to leap on it. "You guys think I could help you?" Flattop asked.

The men looked at him suspiciously. The Robber King leaned forward and squinted at Flattop. "Help us?"

"Yeah . . . I really like horses."

The Robber King raised his eyebrows. "Even the kind that throw up?" He looked at his men and they all burst out laughing. Flattop tried to laugh along, to show he was a good sport.

The Robber King wiped his eyes and sighed. "Very well. 'Twill be easier to keep watch on you." He walked through the bushes on the other side of the clearing with Flattop and the two companions following.

Flattop was glad they let him come, because now he knew there were three horses, not just one. The Robber King's stallion was big—the biggest horse Flattop had ever seen. Horses like that pulled beer wagons in parades—they didn't make good getaway horses. The other two horses were smaller and thinner and probably could get up some speed if they needed to.

With the horses fed, the outlaws got ready for their breakfast. Clumps of dried, stringy, brown stuff were handed out. "Here, lad," the Robber King said as he handed a chunk to Flattop. "I am feeling generous today."

At first, Flattop thought it was nice of him to share their food. Then he remembered they had robbed him. Where he came from, robbers didn't treat their victims to breakfast. But he *was* hungry, so he picked a few strings of meat off and put them in his mouth.

It tasted like pork chops. Actually it tasted like pork chop jerky, which can be pretty delicious when you're starving. After everyone finished the dried meat, the Robber King lifted a big leather pouch and asked Flattop, "Would you care to share our ale, lad?"

Remembering the cider John and Ruth called ale, Flattop nodded yes. He picked strings of pork out of his teeth while he watched the Robber King rummage through a brown linen sack and pull out a cup—a gold cup with red jewels like the one Flattop had seen at the wagon. Visions of the dead, blood-soaked bodies swirled around in his head and made him dizzy. The Robber King filled the cup with ale and handed it to Flattop.

"On second thought," Flattop said, as he put his hands over his eyes and hoped the world would stop spinning, "I'm not thirsty."

"Drink!" the Robber King ordered.

Flattop grabbed the cup and took a big gulp. He felt his throat burn and his eyes bulge out of his head. This ale wasn't cider. Whatever it was, it made his gut churn. He looked at the three men, who happily gulped it down without even having their eyes water.

The Robber King treated himself to seconds and thirds, and finally drank right out of the leather container. It wasn't long before he was in a hazy stupor.

He took off his cloak and spread it on the ground next to the baseball hat that contained the dark glass. He dropped to his knees, crawled onto the cloak and sat down, using the tree trunk as a back rest.

He sighed contentedly, then looked at Flattop. "Where do you come from, lad?"

"California." Flattop knew they wouldn't understand, but it felt good to say it.

"Where are your parents?" the Robber King asked. "And this time, the truth."

Flattop decided not to continue the orphan thing. "I left them."

The Robber King raised his bushy eyebrows. "Why?"

"I wanted an adventure." Possibly because the words were true, they stung even more.

"Well, lad, you must understand," the Robber King said, as he shrugged and looked at his buddies. "Now that you have found us, we cannot let you live."

His buddies nodded solemnly.

"Bind him," the Robber King said with a snarl.

The two companions stood Flattop against a tree and tied his hands around the back with rough, scratchy rope. The Robber King tried to get up, but stumbled back to the ground. He picked up his wooden club in one hand and drew his knife in the other. He looked at both weapons, then shook his head. "I cannot decide. Shall I bash in your head or slit your gullet?"

Flattop swallowed hard and stared at him.

After a long silence, the Robber King sighed, put down both weapons and reached for Flattop's red satin jacket. He settled onto the ground, pulling the jacket over his chest like a blanket and drifted off to sleep. Flattop had to find a way out of this mess before the Robber King woke up.

He looked over to see the two buddies staring at him, whispering and pointing to his clothes. That's when he got the idea for the perfect escape.

"My clothes are kind of funny, huh?" he said.

The two men looked at each other and nodded.

"This is an outfit we wear in California to play a game. Would you like to learn it?"

They shrugged, looked at each other, then nodded again.

"Of course, you'll have to untie me."

One of the men looked worried. "We cannot do that, lad."

"Sure you can. I won't go anywhere."

"I think not," the other one chimed in.

"I'm a kid . . . you know, a child. Where would I go that you couldn't catch me?"

After a moment of whispering, one of the men walked over and untied him. Flattop rubbed his wrists and rolled his shoulders forward a couple times to loosen up.

He tiptoed over to the Robber King, who was now snoring contentedly, and picked up his club. "I'm going to teach you a game called baseball."

Before long, Flattop was tossing a three-inch rock into the air and knocking pop flies with the club. "Now," he said, "I need a pitcher and a catcher." He chose the shorter, heavier guy to be the catcher and showed the taller man how to pitch a ball. Now it was time to put his plan into action.

Last year in the Little League playoffs, he accidentally beaned the Giants' pitcher with a line drive to the head. The kid was knocked out for a good five minutes. Imagine the damage he could do to this guy with a line drive rock. Then all it would take is one good swing of the club and he'd knock the catcher out, too.

He played it nice and easy until the right pitch came sailing toward him, then he swung the club as hard as he could. The next few seconds seemed divided into fractions. He hit the rock. It sped toward the pitcher and made contact with his face. Flattop continued the swing and spun around to deliver a good, hard crack to the side of the catcher's head. In the next instant, both men were unconscious and Flattop was free. He ran to the Robber King's side, picked up his hat and tucked the dark glass into his hip pocket. With one swoop, he grabbed his jacket and turned to run away. That's when the hand grabbed his ankle and sent him toppling to the ground.

"You dirty little thief!" the Robber King bellowed.

Flattop kicked his legs frantically, hoping to get free of the man's grasp, but the Robber King was scrambling toward him on his knees. He still had one big, powerful hand around Flattop's ankle. The other hand gripped his knife, ready to strike as Flattop twisted and squirmed in front of him.

There was no one to call. No police. No superheroes. No mom and dad. Fear and desperation exploded inside his chest. He tried to roll over, hoping to set his leg free, but he only succeeded in flopping onto his back. He saw the reddish purple rage in the Robber King's face.

Images of the murdered family Flattop had found in the wagon flashed through his head. Blood. Arrows. The man slumped in the front seat. The blood-soaked women draped across the back. The dead kid. Stab wounds. Slit throat. The kid. The kid.

The Robber King straddled Flattop, pinning him to the ground. When Flattop tried to wriggle out from under him, the villain pushed down Flattop's shoulder, growled and lifted his knife high above his head. Flattop screamed a gut wrenching "Noooo!" that he was sure would be his last word. His hands dug into the ground. He turned his head and closed his eyes.

The next sound was a strange *tthhhunk.* Then a gasp from the Robber King. Flattop felt him freeze in mid-action. He opened his eyes and looked up to see an arrow sticking out of the center of the Robber King's chest.

The outlaw let the knife fall out of his hand. It bounced in the dirt next to Flattop's arm. The wounded man blinked once, then a horrible gurgle rose out of his throat. He swayed slightly, finally falling forward. The Robber King's chest hit the ground, forcing the arrow all the way through his body. When Flattop saw the blood-soaked tip poke out through the man's back, he let out a terrified howl, then struggled to get out from underneath the dead man. He crawled another twenty feet across the dirt, shaking and gasping for breath, before he could bring himself to look around.

Into the clearing trotted a familiar horse. The gray-hooded rider with the bow in his hand asked, "Are you hurt?"

Flattop looked up into the face of the young squire and shook his head.

# 16

The squire dismounted and draped his bow over his head and across one shoulder. Flattop had seen his sister, Marcia, carry her purse that way, with the shoulder strap stretching diagonally across her chest. On her, it looked stupid. On the squire, it looked pretty cool. The squire pulled a dagger from his belt and ran to the man lying facedown with the blood-drenched arrow sticking through his back.

"He's the Robber King," Flattop blurted out, as he scrambled to retrieve his hat, jacket and the dark glass.

"Aye." The squire pulled the arrow out through the man's back then rolled him over to look at his face. "And dead, at last."

"He was trying to kill me."

"This scoundrel has committed murder and mayhem throughout Lord Hemstead's lands. He has poached the game of this forest and stolen from nobles traveling through the area."

"I know. He tried to take my jacket." Flattop got up, brushed the dirt off his baseball uniform, put on his red satin jacket and tucked the glass into his hip pocket.

"His death will yield me a hefty ransom."

"Ransom?" Flattop had only heard the word ransom used in kidnapping, and it seemed kind of dumb to kidnap a dead guy.

"A reward," the squire explained. "Lord Hemstead has placed a mighty sum on the heads of this varlet and his companions."

"You mean those two guys?" Flattop pointed to the two men still lying unconscious about thirty feet away.

"Sweet Mary!" The squire leapt over the Robber King's body and ran to the bodies of the companions. "Are they dead?"

Flattop started to leap over the Robber King, but was overtaken by a bad case of the creeps. He sidestepped the body and followed the squire. "I knocked 'em out."

"You?" The squire seemed surprised. He knelt by the one Flattop had clobbered with the club and examined the lump on the man's head. "How is't that you overpowered these two outlaws?"

"I used baseball." Flattop shrugged and knelt beside the squire.

"And this . . . 'baseball' . . . be it a new weapon, or a new battle tactic?"

Flattop picked up the club he had used for a bat and smiled. "I guess it's both."

The squire stood up. "We must take these villains to Lord Hemstead before they can recover from your baseball. Have you a horse?"

"No, but they do." Flattop scrambled to his feet and led the squire to the Robber King's three horses.

The squire stroked the long, thick neck of the Robber King's stallion. "This is a hardy steed. A fine reward in itself. Come. I will need your help lashing the men to these horses."

Flattop found a bunch of rope in the Robber King's camping stuff. *Probably used it to tie people up when he robbed them,*

Flattop thought. He had been told that revenge was sweet, and tying up the robbers with their own rope was the sweetest.

Grabbing the legs and arms of the tall, skinny thief, Flattop and the squire hoisted him onto the smallest horse. He lay facedown, draped across the horse's back. Flattop steadied him while the squire secured him to the horse's body. The next guy was a little bigger, but Flattop was already getting the hang of loading unconscious men onto horses' backs.

Getting the Robber King up was messier. His shirt, front and back, was soaked with blood. Flattop took off his jacket so he wouldn't get any stains on it. Just before they picked up the body, Flattop held up his hand. "Wait! My mom gets mad if I come home with grass stains on this shirt. She'd flip if I came home with bloodstains."

He grabbed the Robber King's cloak, which had been lying in a heap beneath the tree, and threw it around his shoulders. Then he and the squire began the task of putting the Robber King on his stallion.

Carrying a dead guy around was kind of like eating broccoli. If Flattop really thought about the bitter taste, the awful smell and the weird texture of those little flowery things rolling around in his mouth, he couldn't swallow a bite of it. But if he didn't think about it, he could gag it down pretty easily. And now, as long as he didn't think about arrows through hearts and the look on the Robber King's face when he died, he could lug the body around without too much trouble.

The squire studied Flattop carefully, watching him flop the dead man's arms on the horse's back, then boosting the lifeless body up. After three tries, they finally got the Robber King's heavy body draped across the saddle. Flattop took off the cloak, draped it over the body, then put his own jacket back on. As they unrolled another length of rope to tie the Robber King to the horse, the squire asked, "What manner of noble are you?"

"Huh?' Flattop would've gladly answered the question if he knew what it meant.

"What is your name?"

"Flattop Kincaid."

The squire paused for a moment, looking very puzzled. "Are you Norman?"

"No, I'm Marvin." Flattop corrected him, wondering how this guy came up with a dumber name than Marvin.

"You do not come from the Norman region of France?" the squire asked.

Flattop's brain clicked into high gear. He remembered that John had thought he was from France because his clothes were different and he talked funny. If it worked before, it might work again. "Yeah," he said casually, "I come from France."

"But you are not from the area known as Normandy?"

"Nope." Flattop shook his head. "I'm from the area known as California."

The squire and Flattop grabbed all the sacks containing the Robber King's loot and fastened them to the saddle of the big, black steed. "Fetch my horse," the squire said to Flattop.

When Flattop returned, the squire was tying the outlaws' horses into a single file line. He held the rope and climbed into the saddle. Extending a hand down to Flattop, he said, "Come up, then."

Flattop had no idea how to get on a horse that already had a rider. The squire pulled his foot partway out of the stirrup and pointed to it. "Step here." Flattop put his foot on top of the squire's, took hold of his hand, and in one smooth, upward move, found himself seated behind the high-backed, wooden saddle, right on the horse's rump.

The squire handed the rope to Flattop and smiled. "See

to our prisoners." Flattop nodded and held the rope tightly. They led the solemn procession out of the forest, the two smaller horses each carrying one of the companions and the last horse, the big, powerful stallion carrying the body of the Robber King.

Flattop didn't want to slide off the back of the horse, so he put his arms around the squire's midsection. He rode on the back of his uncle's motorcycle once, but he didn't feel stupid hanging onto his uncle.

"What's your name?" Flattop figured a conversation might make him feel more comfortable.

"I am called William." The squire straightened in his saddle. "However, I may be known as *Sir* William when Lord Hemstead sees what I have done."

"What difference does *sir* make?" Flattop asked.

" 'Tis my hope that Lord Hemstead will show his gratitude by dubbing me."

"Dubbing you?" Flattop asked.

"Aye. Making me a knight."

What luck! Flattop had only been in the Middle Ages a couple days and already he might get the chance to see a guy get knighted. Things were definitely looking up. He bet his dad never had an adventure like this.

There was no sound except the rustle of wet leaves as the horses trudged along the forest path. Flattop saw tiny streams of light filter through the trees and collect on the ground like pools of water. And to think, only a couple of hours ago he was chasing through the forest, following the cry of the hawk.

*The hawk! Where's the hawk?*

"Hey, William." He tried to sound indifferent. "Where's your hawk?"

"Oh, you mean Millesande? She is in the mews."

"You didn't bring her with you?" Flattop asked.

"No, I was not hunting today. At least, not for game. I had to patrol Lord Hemstead's forest."

Finally they emerged from the moist darkness of the forest into the mid-morning sunlight. The sun warmed up the wet fields and made the air damp and sticky. Flattop looked around at the scenery—at all the sights he would've never seen again if the Robber King had had his way only a short while ago. "William?"

"Aye?"

Flattop tried to think of the right words to say, but all that came out was, "I just wanted to thank you . . . for . . . you know . . . saving my life and everything."

"You are welcome," was the simple reply.

Squire William's horse followed the river bank toward the castle. Flattop looked over to see a familiar hut standing alone. He saw John, Ruth and Margaret gouging trenches in the dirt while Catherine and Little George followed behind, sprinkling seed and chasing away the birds.

*They're serfs*, the Wizard had said. *That's what their life is like.* Endless days of backbreaking work, and even that might not prevent them from starving to death. Flattop thought about John and Ruth's two kids who'd died. He tried to imagine the family without Margaret. Or Catherine. Or Little George. Ruth was right to try to get Margaret placed in the castle. Even if she just ate garbage, she'd be better off than she was now.

John was the first to notice the string of horses being led to the castle. Then Ruth and the kids looked up. Flattop risked tumbling off the horse's behind to wave at them. They looked at one another, then looked away. Only Little George raised a hand to wave back. Ruth rushed to his side and pushed his hand down.

Flattop took in a quick breath of air and was ready to call out, "Hey, you guys! Look, it's me! Flattop!" That's when he remembered how afraid they were of the knight and his squire. He relived yesterday's nightmare, when John smacked him to the ground and ordered him to leave the family because he'd get them all thrown in the dungeon. Getting attention, even from the kid who helped capture the Robber King and his men, meant getting into trouble.

They preferred to remain invisible.

Flattop put his arm down and turned his head away from the family that had fed him, clothed him and given him a place to sleep. He had lost two families now, and the empty place in his heart had gotten a little bigger.

Tears welled in his eyes, but if he raised his hand to wipe them away, William would know he was crying like a stupid baby. He closed his eyelids and raised his head toward the sun, thinking maybe evaporation might do the trick. But all he felt was two tiny trickles of water run from his eyes into his ears.

"What business do you have with Lord Hemstead's serfs?" Squire William asked.

"Huh?" Flattop opened his eyes and wiped the sides of his face on his jacket.

"The serfs in yonder field. You waved to them. I hope you hold no plan to steal these workers who have pledged their loyalty to Lord Hemstead."

"No." Flattop was shocked to hear this guy talk about stealing people like they were VCRs or something. "They helped me, that's all. I just wanted to thank them."

"Worthless serfs helping a noble such as yourself?" The squire chuckled. "You have a ready wit."

Flattop scowled, offended by William's snobby attitude. He decided to try his poor-little-orphan story once more. "My parents and I were traveling on vacation. One of our horses got sick and he was . . . well . . . he wasn't throwing up, but he was sick."

"Yes . . . continue."

"Well, we stopped to fix the horse and the Robber King came out of the forest." Flattop paused to cross his fingers. "He killed my mom and dad. Then he knocked me on the head and robbed us. That family over there found me."

"Probably hoping for a reward."

"They knew I didn't have anything, but they took care of me anyway. And they're really poor. They eat porridge all the time and—"

"Provided by the generosity and charity of Lord Hemstead," the squire interrupted.

"Hey, they work hard for that guy. I know. I helped 'em yesterday and my back still hurts."

The squire stopped his horse and sat perfectly still for a few seconds. Then he turned around in his saddle to look at Flattop's face. "Was it you who chased my hawk back to me?"

"Yeah." *Duh*, thought Flattop.

The squire faced front again and, with a flick of the reins, urged his horse forward. "But you were wearing rags."

Flattop sighed. "I know. Little George wet the bed and got these clothes all wet. So they let me wear some of their stuff till my stuff dried."

"This family has served you well."

"I know. I just wanted to thank them."

The squire shook his head. "You are a noble. It is their duty to attend you."

Flattop started to argue then realized it wouldn't do any good. William acted like John and Ruth lived on another planet—like they weren't human beings. Flattop sighed. Yesterday, William seemed like such a nice guy—especially compared to that pushy knight. And today he had saved Flattop's life. It was disappointing to hear him talk like a jerk now.

They rode in silence for several minutes, a somber parade of horses and bad guys. A groan from the man tied to the second horse made Flattop and William turn around to check on their prisoners.

" 'Tis a good thing we are almost to the castle," the squire said. "These varlets will be coming around soon."

Flattop looked over his shoulder at the bodies slung across the horses' backs. He tried to ignore the Robber King on the last horse, but he kept catching glimpses of the dead man's face.

"You must tell me more about this 'baseball.' " William paused for a moment. "You say it is a new battle tactic?"

"No." Flattop smiled. "It's a game."

"Heavens! In California, you make a game of bashing people in the head?"

Flattop laughed. "No. We play a game called baseball. We hit a ball with a bat and then we—"

"Is the bat dead?"

It took Flattop a moment to figure out where the conversation had taken a wrong turn. He smiled and shook his head. "Not the animal. A piece of wood . . . like a club." The mental picture of a baseball player swinging a dead bat at home plate struck him as one of the funniest things he'd ever seen and he started laughing. "A bat! I'm sure!"

He saw the squire's back stiffen and his head raise. Obviously, this guy had no sense of humor. "Hey, come on, William, you gotta admit it would look pretty dumb."

William started to chuckle. "I suppose the bat would not fancy it much, either." Both of them enjoyed a good laugh over that.

By the time they arrived at the castle, a crowd had lined the drawbridge to watch.

"Behold!" shouted William. "We have slain the Robber King!"

People scurried about, whispering to their neighbors.

"Make way for the body of the Robber King!" William called out to the throng of people gathering in front of him. Flattop was a little embarrassed that William was making such a big production out of this.

But as they made their way through the mob, Flattop started to hear applause, and the whispers changed to rousing cheers. They turned down the alley and headed toward the cookhouse.

"The Robber King shall prey on us no more!" William called to the people spilling out of their shops and stables.

Above the noise in the alley, Flattop heard church bells ringing wildly. His embarrassment was turning into joy. *This must be what it feels like to be in the Rose Parade*, he thought. As they rounded a corner, Flattop got into the spirit of things and waved to the seemingly endless line of fans.

William raised his head and shouted to the guards on the top of the castle wall. "The Robber King and his accomplices shall ride no more!" His voice bounced off the jagged stone edges of the high walls.

Flattop was just about to yell, "We showed these guys a thing or two!" when he saw a familiar door straight ahead. *The mews. The hawk house.* Apparently, the alley made a complete circle. He wanted to get off the horse and see the Wizard, but he would never be able to explain it to William. Flattop never took his eyes off the hawk house door. Not even after they had passed it and slowly approached the last turn of the circular alley.

For Flattop, the noise of the crowd became muffled. All he heard was his own heart, beating faster and louder as they rode on. He took one hand off William's midsection

**101**

and reached into his back pocket to feel the smooth edges of the dark glass. As the horses rounded the last corner, something soft and cool hit him in the face. He turned around to see a toothless woman throwing flowers at him. He took his hand out of his pocket to wave at her. He'd have to see the Wizard later.

They arrived back at the entrance, but instead of making a left turn out to the drawbridge, William made a right turn and guided the procession across another drawbridge over another moat. *Hmm,* Flattop thought as he looked down into the smelly, brown water. *A castle within a castle.*

The gate at the other end opened, and a bearded, round man wearing a dark red tunic stepped forward and struck a majestic pose to the left of their horse. He tugged at the lapels of a big, fur-trimmed coat that looked like a cross between a robe and a cloak.

A grumpy-looking woman followed closely behind. Her head was covered with a hood like the one Little George wore, but she was definitely not a peasant. Her dark blue, floor-length tunic had jewels and gold on it and she had a coat with red fur trim.

*Holy cow!* thought Flattop. *They must be some kind of king and queen!* He remembered reading somewhere that when meeting royalty, men are supposed to bow—women curtsy. He had to bow after a school play once. *One arm in front, one in back, bend at the waist.* He was pleased that he was prepared.

He felt an elbow jab the front of his ribs and heard William whisper, "Dismount!" Flattop handed him the rope, stuck his right foot in the stirrup and dropped down to the heavy wood planking on the drawbridge. It wasn't until he heard a little kid giggle that he realized he was standing on the wrong side of the horse.

He didn't want to walk in front of the horse because he'd bump into the grouchy queen, and he couldn't walk in back because he might get kicked, so he quickly ran the length of all four horses, his cleats rattling along the beams of the bridge.

*White makes my steps sure and true. A Red Sox player is fast of foot.*

He rounded the last horse, giving it ample kicking room, then raced toward William.

*Men bow, women curtsy.*

"My Lord," William said, "I deliver to you the body of the Robber King."

*One arm in front, one in back, bend at the waist.*

With that, Squire William bowed his head and knelt, touching one knee to the floor.

Flattop was scrambling to a stop, thinking, *That's not a bow! That's not a bow!*

The nobleman looked at Flattop, who was panting furiously from his wind sprint around the four horses. "And who might this lad be?" the king asked.

Squire William quickly stood up. "This lad disabled the Robber King's men and afforded me a clean strike to the villain's heart." William proudly extended a hand toward Flattop. "Lord Hemstead, may I present to you, Flattop Kincaid."

*Lord Hemstead? He's not a king? Do I bow before a lord?*

Flattop stepped forward, tightly gripping the bottom of his satin jacket. He started to bow, then tried to put his knee on the ground like the squire had done. When he flung his arms out to help him balance, he executed a perfect curtsy. He heard several gasps from the crowd.

"Forgive him, my lord," William said. "He is from California."

## 18

Flattop held the curtsy for a long time, hoping the earth might open up and swallow him. There had to be five hundred people watching him, and he messed everything up. A stupid curtsy! He felt his face get hot and tingly and he knew that it was probably redder than his jacket. He stared at the thick wooden beams beneath his feet.

After an uneasy silence, Lord Hemstead tossed his head back in a hearty laugh and the rest of the crowd joined in. "Welcome, Master Flattop," the man said as he slapped Flattop on the back. "My wife and I will be honored to have you and Squire William share our table this day."

"Cool," Flattop replied. "I mean, thank you . . . uh . . . lord."

"*My* lord," William said, correcting him.

"*My* lord," echoed Flattop.

Lord Hemstead walked over to face William. "As for you, lad, your skill and bravery in dispatching the Robber King and his evil band have proven you worthy of knighthood. We will begin preparations for your dubbing."

The crowd applauded and cheered. Little kids jumped up and down. Flattop got hit in the face with some more flowers.

William took a step back as though the words had knocked him off balance. Then, bowing his head, he knelt before Lord and Lady Hemstead. "I remain your humble servant, my lord."

"Come, then!" Lord Hemstead commanded. "Let us make our brave young heroes comfortable." He turned to his wife and ordered, "Woman, see to it that William and Flattop are given our finest chamber. I will dispatch a messenger requesting Lord Wickshire's presence at his brother's dubbing."

"Aye, my lord." Lady Hemstead nodded, then turned to William and Flattop. "Come with me, good sirs." She led them across the courtyard to the tall stone tower on the other side.

Flattop tried to be friendly. "Nice place you got here."

But Lady Hemstead just kept scowling and walking. It didn't take long for Flattop to figure out that she was one of those people who was grouchy all the time. He made a mental note to stay out of her way.

She started up the narrow wooden stairs that wound around the outside of the castle tower to a door halfway up. William fell in step behind her and Flattop followed.

"Where's she taking us?" Flattop whispered to William.

"To the *donjon*."

Flattop's mouth dropped open. "The dungeon?" He'd seen old movies about people rotting in dungeons. People with big rats crawling across their chained bodies. People who breathed their last in cold, slimy underground torture chambers. For a fleeting moment he acknowledged to himself that Lady Hemstead was leading them *up*stairs, not down. But he didn't have time to argue over small details. Maybe he could still get away. He looked around nervously and rubbed his sweaty palms on his baseball pants.

"What troubles you, Flattop?" William asked.

"Don't you know what a dungeon is? It's a prison."

"Perhaps it is in California, but here it is what we call this building." William slapped the stone wall as he continued to climb the steps.

Flattop ran his hand along the uneven chunks of rock. "This whole thing is a dungeon?"

"*Don . . . jon,* yes," said William very slowly for Flattop's benefit. "It is the safest, most protected structure in all of Lord Hemstead's castle."

Flattop grabbed the wobbly wooden railing. "These stairs don't seem very safe."

"Goodness, no. They have to come down quickly," William said over his shoulder as they continued to climb.

"What do you mean?" Flattop asked.

"Let us suppose the castle is under attack by a larger and more powerful enemy and we are facing defeat. Our last stronghold is the donjon. We climb the stairs, then release them from the building. Lord Hemstead and all of his forces are safe."

"What about those big doors downstairs?"

"Grain storage." William smiled. "These stairs are the only access to the living quarters."

Flattop nodded his approval. "Pretty tricky."

"Where is it that you find safety within your castle?" William asked.

Flattop thought for a minute as he trudged up the creaky wooden steps. "I guess it'd be the bathroom. You can lock the door if your sister's chasing you, or something."

When Lady Hemstead hesitated and looked over her shoulder at him, he forced a fake laugh and quickly added, "Just kidding."

At the top of the stairs, Lady Hemstead pushed open the heavy wood and iron door and walked in. Flattop and William followed. Flattop immediately stumbled over a pile of dried-up leaves and stems. He looked ahead to discover more of them, heaped a couple layers thick, all over the floor.

Flattop pushed through the leaves with his toe. "Wow! What a mess! Who takes care of this?"

Lady Hemstead stopped walking and turned around to give him an icy stare. "The new *rushes* will be laid at the next full moon, young man. And not a moment sooner." She turned around, stuck out her chin and walked away.

Flattop was off to a rotten start with her. "I didn't mean to hurt your feelings or anything," he called out. "We don't have these bushes at my . . . uh . . . castle."

"They're called *rushes*," William whispered. "We harvest them from the marshes and lay them on the floors once a year. Otherwise, the stone floors can become very cold during the winter. Do you not have a way to keep your castle floors warm in California?"

"Sure. We call it carpeting."

"Come, sirs," Lady Hemstead directed, taking the lead again.

Flattop took his mind off the rushes and looked around. He was in a big room filled with long, straight rows of heavy, wooden tables like the one John had. Wooden picnic-type benches were placed on both sides of the tables. Except for the high ceiling and the rainbow of colorful banners that hung overhead, it looked kind of like his school cafeteria.

He stopped for a moment and pictured the kids at school eating pizza and burritos at these tables, trading Tater Tots for chocolate milk or swapping canned peaches for someone's cookies. Another twinge of sadness stung him. Now he was even homesick for school.

He snapped out of his sorrow when he felt something bump his leg. Two skinny, flop-eared dogs brushed past as they wandered through the room, pushing their noses through the stems and twigs on the floor.

"Hey, look!" Flattop said, smiling. "Dogs." He bent down

107

to pet the brown-and-white one who was crunching on a bone under one of the benches. That's when he saw the bigger, black-and-brown dog jump on top of one of the tables to lick the food scraps and juices off.

"No!" Flattop scolded. "Get down! Bad dog!"

The black-and-brown dog never even looked up.

"Aren't you going to make him get down?" Flattop asked Lady Hemstead.

"How do you think I keep my tables so clean?" she replied with a shrug.

Flattop watched as the brown-and-white dog leaped on a table and hungrily forced his tongue down into the cracks between the wooden planks. Flattop winced. Pizza World wasn't always the cleanest place, but at least they used soapy water to clean the tables—not dog slobber.

William looked fondly around the room. "This is where I usually sleep."

"Here?" Flattop asked.

William nodded. "This is the Great Hall. All the knights, squires and pages who aren't family members or honored guests sleep in here on the tables."

Flattop wondered if beds had been invented yet. He thought about his nights in John's hut, sleeping on a straw mattress that had been flopped on the tabletop. Stinky bodies. Snoring. Bed-wetting. And that had only been five other people. He tried to imagine what it would be like, sleeping in the same room with a whole bunch of guys.

"Let us proceed," Lady Hemstead ordered. She went out the double doors on the other side of the Great Hall and disappeared down a corridor. Flattop and William hurried to catch up with her. The hallway was dark and cold. The only light came from the thick, yellowish candles that burned in holders on the wall.

Flattop noticed that the whole place, including the hallway, smelled like McDonald's. Someone was frying up hamburgers somewhere and the smell made his mouth water. That's when he realized he hadn't eaten anything since that beef-soaked bread at John's house the day before. His stomach growled, echoing down the stone corridor. Lady Hemstead turned around to look at him again.

He grabbed his stomach. "Sorry. I guess I'm pretty hungry."

"Shall I fetch you something from the cookhouse?" she asked.

"No." Flattop shook his head, not wanting to be a bother. But another stomach growl changed his mind. "Well, maybe an apple or something."

"I do not think we will have any cooked just yet."

"Oh, that's okay," he told her. "I can eat one raw."

Both William and Lady Hemstead stopped walking and turned around to stare at him. Flattop had done it again—although he wasn't sure what he'd done.

"You cannot be serious," said William.

Lady Hemstead scowled. "I would never serve uncooked fruit, sir. It is vile and poisonous and not fit for my most despised enemy." She whirled around and continued to walk down the hall—but at a faster pace.

It suddenly occurred to Flattop that she had no trouble giving peasants food that she thought was poisonous. Just yesterday, he had savored apple and pear cores right down to the seeds. He wanted to tell her that, but he had a pretty good idea that it would sound rude, no matter how nice he tried to say it. So he decided to keep his mouth shut.

"Here is your chamber." Lady Hemstead opened a door on her left and gestured for William and Flattop to enter.

Flattop was relieved to discover that beds *had* been invented and that a rather large one was right in the middle of his new bedroom. Four thick wooden posts rose up like telephone poles from the four corners. They attached to a wooden frame about eight feet above the bed. Heavy burgundy fabric was draped over the top and tied with gold cord.

On the far wall, between two candles, hung a big woven rug with a fancy green and brown design. Underneath it stood a dark brown wooden chest with detailed carvings on the side. Lady Hemstead walked to a small adjoining room and patted a huge barrel.

"We shall provide you with a bath immediately," she said. "And I shall be on my way." As though on cue, a parade of servants—old, young, male and female—came through the door. Each had a bucket of water to toss into the wooden barrel.

"What are they doing?" Flattop asked.

"Preparing our bath." William set his gloves down on the bed and pulled back his gray hood to unleash wild, curly locks of chestnut brown hair that fell forward around his face. "I shall go first," he announced.

Flattop circled around the tub, inspecting it. He watched servant after servant pour in buckets of water. "How long will I have to wait for them to get my bath ready?"

"There is only one bath, Flattop. I shall go first and you will follow me."

"You want me to take a bath in *your water?*" Flattop asked.

"It will still be warm."

"That's gross!" Flattop said. "It'll be dirty and—" Flattop stopped in mid-sentence. Lady Hemstead was scowling at him again, so he tried to be a better guest and look on the bright side. He already had lice and fleas. What more could happen? Besides, it was kind of like being in a Jacuzzi with a lot of other people. Kind of.

Flattop agreed to be second in the tub, then went to lie down on the big bed. The mattress sank under his weight and smelled like a chicken coop. As he rolled onto his stomach, a tiny feather poofed out of the mattress. *Down-filled,*

110

thought Flattop. Just like his ski jacket at home. The bed gave way so easily, Flattop felt like he was being swallowed. He closed his eyes and tried not to think of the grayish soap-and-dirt scum he left in his bathtub at home.

A host of images flashed through his brain. His mom and dad. The swap meet. John and his family. The hawk. The bloody arrow sticking out of the Robber King's chest. The Wizard's face in the dark glass. The dogs licking the table.

Nothing was like he thought it would be. The rich people were snobs and the poor people—he'd never really thought about how the poor people would have to live. Come to think of it, he never thought about how the poor people had to live in his own century. Maybe he was nothing more than a modern-day snobby noble.

Oh, sure, he brought canned food to school at Thanksgiving and Christmas so they could have a nice holiday dinner, but he never really thought about how the poor people ate the rest of the year. He decided that from now on, he'd bring more food—better food. No more grabbing a can of beans off the kitchen shelf. Maybe he'd give them ravioli. He loved ravioli. And a six-pack of Dr. Pepper. That would be much better. He closed his eyes and imagined alternating mouthfuls of ravioli and Dr. Pepper.

In what seemed like the next instant, William was shaking him awake. "Flattop, you must bathe, then make ready for dinner in the Great Hall."

Flattop did his best to clear the cobwebs out of his brain and struggle out of bed. He took off his clothes and leaped into the tub quickly, refusing to look at the secondhand bath water.

After deciding not to wash his face or hair, he got out and looked for a towel. The only thing available was a big piece of linen cloth. It was like drying off with a bedsheet, but it would have to do. Then he began putting on his baseball uniform. *Red sleeves mean a Red Sox player has powerful arms,* he thought to himself as he put on his T-shirt and jersey.

A young girl who looked about Margaret's age came in and Flattop practically tripped over his pants trying to get both legs in at the same time. The girl didn't seem to notice. She stooped down and glanced inside a large clay container, then turned around and left.

"Who's she?" Flattop asked.

William shrugged. "One of the chambermaids, checking our pot."

Flattop walked over and looked down past the pour spout. "Anything good to drink in there?"

"Goodness, no!" said William. "Do you not know what this is for?"

"Iced tea?" asked Flattop with a shrug.

"It is to relieve yourself after a long ride, or in the middle of the night."

"Relieve myself?" Flattop wasn't sure he heard that right. "What the heck do I need relief—ohhhhhhhh!" It dawned on him. William was talking about going to the bathroom in that . . . thing. And then giving it to some little seven-year-old girl. He cringed at the thought.

Maybe it was time to take another bathroom oath.

"Come, Flattop," William said as he opened the bedchamber door. "We are the guests of honor."

"I'm coming," Flattop replied. He pulled his baseball cap down onto his forehead and mumbled to himself, "Red means a Red Sox player outthinks his opponents." He'd been wearing his cap for a couple days straight now, and he still couldn't outthink the Wizard. Maybe Coach Hartman's dressing ceremony was a lot of baloney.

"Come, Flattop," William repeated. "We must not be late."

Flattop started toward the door then remembered his mom saying it was rude to come to the dinner table wearing a hat, so he grabbed the bill, flung it through the air like a Frisbee and watched it land in the middle of the bed. Then he followed William out the door and into the hallway.

The candles on the wall flickered and threw dancing shadows on the ceiling. It made Flattop feel like he was in an old Frankenstein movie. He probably would've been a little scared but he smelled that McDonald's smell again. He didn't think hamburgers had been invented yet, but there was no harm in checking.

"Hey, William, you ever eaten a hamburger?" Flattop asked.

"I have eaten *ham* many times," William offered.

"No." Flattop shook his head. "It's not the same thing." He wondered how long human beings would have to wait for a good burger.

As he followed William down the steps to the Great Hall, Flattop felt a jab in his hip. The purple glass was at an uncomfortable angle in his back pocket and the corner poked him with every step. He stopped for a minute to straighten it.

"Hey, William. You ever heard of wizards?"

William stopped and looked up at Flattop. "Aye," he replied cautiously. "I have heard."

"Well, do you believe in them?" Flattop was tired of lying to everyone and he figured William would be a perfect person to confide in. Except for his snobby attitude about serfs, he was pretty cool.

"Do I believe in wizards?" William repeated, then started down the stairs again, this time more slowly. "Absolutely."

Flattop's heart soared. At last, he could share his secret.

"I believe in sorcerers, conjurors, witches and wizards," William continued. "They are all demons who will rob you of your very soul and send you plunging, naked, into the depths of Hades." William stopped at the bottom of the steps and turned to Flattop. "Why do you ask?"

Flattop shrugged. "I just wondered." It looked like he'd have to keep his secret a little longer.

Flattop heard a scuffling sound and a couple of growls from the stairs above him. The two dogs he had seen earlier stampeded past, knocking Flattop and William against the stone wall. The black-and-brown dog barked and wagged its tail as it raced to catch up with its buddy.

"You must forgive our hounds," William said, smiling. "I am afraid food is their only concern now."

114

Flattop started to nod in agreement when a drop of melted wax from a candle overhead landed on his ear. He let out a yelp, then reached up to grab whatever was burning his skin. He rubbed the quickly cooling wax between his fingers, then held it to his nose and sniffed. "Hamburgers," he said, amazed.

"*These* are hamburgers?" William asked. "Are you suggesting we eat them?"

"No." Flattop shook his head. "They *smell* like hamburgers. You know . . . beef?"

William smiled. "Oh. Of course they do. They are made from tallow—animal fat."

"You make candles out of beef fat?" Flattop asked, scraping the hardened wax from his fingers.

"Or pork or lamb fat. Whatever is plentiful."

Flattop wasn't sure what modern candles were made of, but they smelled like pine trees or flowers, never like burgers.

At the doorway of the Great Hall, William and Flattop paused, preparing to make their entrance as Lord Hemstead's guests of honor. Flattop tucked in his shirt and smoothed the wrinkles out. His father always said, "You get one chance to make a good first impression," and Flattop didn't want to blow it. He wished the Wizard were here to help him, but he'd just have to fake it, like he had done with everything else in the Middle Ages. He took a deep breath, entered the room and stood next to William.

There must've been fifty people standing around the long wooden tables talking to each other. The men wore tunics and stretchy knit pants that looked like something a girl would wear. All the ladies wore long dresses with big, pointy sleeves that hung down from their wrists. The bright blues, yellows and greens were a nice change from the drab browns that John's family wore.

Torches blazed in iron holders along the stone walls, giving everything a warm, orange glow. The black smoke that rose from them clouded the room, but no one seemed to mind.

In front of the huge fireplace, five musicians played softly. Two had little guitarlike instruments, one played the tambourine and two more blew into recorders made of reddish-brown polished wood. Flattop had learned to play the recorder in his sixth grade music appreciation class, but the only song he ever mastered was "Twinkle, Twinkle, Little Star," and he still squeaked on a few of the notes.

He felt a little twinge of fear when he saw the pushy knight laughing and talking across the room. "Hey, William," Flattop said, trying to sound calm. "There's your friend."

William shook his head. "He is not my friend. He is Sir Humphrey, the knight I serve."

"What do you have to do for him?" Flattop asked.

"I care for his horse and armor. In return, he teaches me the skills I need to become a knight."

"Like working with hawks?" Flattop asked.

"Aye." William looked at Flattop and smiled. "And becoming an expert marksman with a bow."

Just then, Sir Humphrey looked up, caught Flattop staring at him and walked over. Flattop's heart pounded in fear. He looked down and moved the toe of his cleats through the rushes on the floor. Maybe if he said he was sorry for staring—

"William!" Sir Humphrey called out. "I am proud of you!" He wasn't mad, after all. Sir Humphrey slapped his right hand into William's and held on. Flattop noticed it was like a handshake without the shaking part. Sir Humphrey turned to Flattop. "And this is the brave young noble who assisted you today?"

"Aye," William answered. "This is Flattop Kincaid."

Flattop stood up straight, faced the knight and clasped his

hand. Sir Humphrey's grip was so tight, Flattop thought his fingers might break.

"Nice to meet you," Flattop said through the pain.

He waited for Sir Humphrey to say something about almost knocking him into the moat and threatening him with a sword, but all he did was congratulate them and walk away.

Sir Humphrey didn't even recognize him. That's when Flattop remembered that yesterday he was dressed like a serf. Yesterday he hadn't been considered a human being.

"Ah, here they are!" Lord Hemstead's voice boomed above the music and conversation, snapping Flattop out of his sadness. "Lords and ladies, William and Flattop have arrived." Everyone applauded. "Let us take our seats." He motioned for his two guests of honor to follow him to the head table, which was up on a decorated platform. Flattop remembered his cousin Nancy's wedding reception, where the bride and groom sat at a table like this. They seemed to like it, but he felt awkward being put on display.

Once everyone was seated, Lord Hemstead gave a little speech welcoming William and Flattop. Then he clapped his hands three times and ordered the food to be served. With that, the doors to the Great Hall swung open and in walked a parade of servants carrying platters of food.

Flattop's tongue was practically hanging out of his mouth as the aroma of ham and roast beef wafted by. First, a young boy came around and plopped a big, thick slice of bread on the table. Serving girls followed, placing meats, vegetables and gravy on the top of the bread.

"Hey, William," Flattop whispered, "they forgot the plates."

"You do not need one with a trencher. The bread serves as your plate."

Flattop nodded, then took another look at the sauce and meats piled on the bread before him. He'd seen chili served inside a big, round crusty bread once, but this was a little different. Definitely messier. He picked up the crudely hammered metal spoon, took a taste and smiled. No doubt about it, this had porridge beat.

Yesterday in the cookhouse, Flattop had seen the meat hiss and drop on an open grill. He guessed that's what gave the beef its smoky, barbecued taste.

When his portion was finished, he picked up the bread to tear off a chunk. William grabbed his hand.

"Do not eat the bread. It is given to the serfs."

Flattop's mouth dropped open. This was the beef-soaked bread he had eaten with John's family last night. After it had served its purpose as a plate, the bread was thrown to the serfs. The thought didn't exactly disgust him, but it made him sad. Nice, hardworking people like John and Ruth and their kids were truly eating garbage.

He thought about the two dogs that had licked the tables clean. The odds were very good that the trencher he had eaten was covered with dog spit. Flattop was glad he discovered all this after he finished eating, because now he'd lost his appetite. When dessert was presented, Flattop said, "No, thank you," hoping Margaret might be able to collect on a whole baked pear to share with her family.

People talked and laughed and ate for what seemed like hours. Flattop told Lord and Lady Hemstead his poor-orphan story, remembering to cross his fingers at the part where the Robber King kills his parents. Lady Hemstead put her hand to her mouth and shook her head in horror. Lord Hemstead got mad at the Robber King all over again.

"That accursed varlet!" He pounded his hand on the table, then pushed his chair out, stood up and raised his cup of ale. The entire room got quiet. Even the dogs stopped fighting over the bone they'd found in the rushes.

"Until today, we have been plagued by a villain most foul. He has plundered our forest of its game, robbed the good nobles who traveled our land and murdered the fine, loving parents of this young lad." He gestured toward Flattop, then paused like the school principal always did when he wanted to make a point.

"But this fiend shall no longer prey upon the good people of Hemstead. For this courageous lad, Flattop Kincaid, seeking revenge for the death of his parents, sought out the Robber King and his vile band of thieves." He paused again, turned and gestured grandly toward William.

"And this young man, our very own Squire William, who was also bravely seeking the head of the Robber King, put an arrow in his bow and, with aim sure and true, did pierce the very heart of the villain."

A huge cheer rose from all the people at the tables. Everyone stood and raised their glasses to the two heroes of the hour.

Lord Hemstead continued, "I salute you, Flattop, for your sense of duty to your slain parents and for your courage in the face of death. And William, your skill, bravery and loyalty to me have earned you knighthood. I drink to your dubbing, when you shall arise *Sir* William."

The people at the tables went crazy. They cheered and drank and hugged one another. The musicians played louder and faster, and everyone got up to dance. Flattop saw both dogs jump on the table and start lapping up slopped-over beef and gravy.

Somehow, all the noise and laughter made Flattop feel lonely. Maybe he had lied one too many times about his parents getting killed. Maybe it bothered him that he was an outsider. Whatever it was, it left him with a big, hollow feeling right in the middle of his stomach. And watching everyone else have such a good time just made it worse.

When he was sure that everyone was wrapped up in the party and wouldn't notice he was gone, he slipped outside and tiptoed away.

## ●●●●●●
# 20

The castle had been so dark inside that Flattop was surprised to find it was still light outside. He squinted against the brightness the way he had to when he left a movie theater after a matinee. He checked his watch. Three o'clock. Today he'd already helped kill a guy, knocked two others out, taken a disgusting bath and gotten a hero's welcome in a real, live castle. Things sure happened fast in the Middle Ages.

Back in his century, he'd be walking home from school right now, complaining about all the homework he had to do. But homework was easy, compared to planting seeds all day. Then he would be facing the nightly struggle against his parents' insistence that he eat his peas, or spinach, or whatever disgusting vegetable they piled on his plate. Visions of green beans with almonds flashed through his brain.

Then something weird happened. The green beans didn't look so bad, after all. In fact, when he got home, he'd ask his mom to make some. He stopped for a moment, puzzled by his sudden attitude change about vegetables. Maybe that's what two days of porridge did to a person.

He began a mental list of all the foods he'd ever refused

to eat and decided to reconsider them. *Carrots? Maybe. Peas? Yes. Broccoli? Broccoli? Maybe not right away. Mushrooms?* An involuntary shudder traveled through his neck and shoulders. Maybe he shouldn't rush this whole vegetable thing. He'd start with green beans and see where it led him.

He wandered across the inner drawbridge and took a walk down the alley. Before he knew it, he was standing in front of the hawk house—the mews. "Millesande," he said to himself. William's hawk, the one the Wizard was using as a hiding place, was in the mews.

Flattop looked up and down the alley, making sure no one saw him, then he flung open the door, slipped inside and pulled the door closed again. A couple of the birds got startled when he ran in so quickly. They flapped around their cages and squawked. But Millesande sat almost motionless on the highest perch, quietly watching his every move.

The room was dark except for the sunlight shining through the cracks between the wooden planks of the walls. Flattop walked to Millesande's cage. He wanted to look in her eyes and see the Wizard there, but she remained on her perch high above his head.

"Wizard? Hey, it's me." The bird didn't move. "I helped catch the Robber King today." Flattop scuffed the straw on the floor with his shoe. "It's a pretty big deal around here. They're still dancing over it upstairs."

The hawk tilted her head and continued to stare down at him. "The thing is," Flattop continued, "I did a big, heroic thing and—" He paused and looked down at his shoes, embarrassed and half-ashamed at what he was going to ask. "I was wondering if that might be enough to get me out of here."

He heard the ruffle of the hawk's wings, then the clink of her talons on the metal cage. Flattop looked up. Millesande was clinging to the cage, staring at him. He studied the hawk's piercing eyes and his heart sank. The Wizard was gone.

Flattop left the mews and wandered farther down the alley. He checked his watch. Three-thirty. John and his family would be coming home from a day in the fields. Coming home to reheated porridge—and garbage, if they were lucky. Meanwhile, up in the Great Hall, dogs were standing on the tables and eating everything in sight.

Suddenly, Flattop knew what he had to do. He ran back through the alley, past the mews, over the inner drawbridge and up the stairs of the donjon. When he walked into the Great Hall, he was relieved to see the party still going strong.

He pushed through the maze of dancers until he found Lord and Lady Hemstead. They had been so moved by the made-up story of his parents' deaths, maybe they would be moved by the true story of the way John and Ruth had taken care of him. He told them of how John carried him to the hut when he was first found and how Ruth gave him medicine to help him recover. He asked Lord and Lady Hemstead if he could please take some of the food scraps to John's family. They instructed a serving girl to take Flattop to the cookhouse and prepare a sack of food.

In less than an hour, Flattop was running up the big hill toward John's house. Twisted around each hand were linen sacks of ham, beef, vegetables, bread and cooked pears. When he saw their hut on the other side of the hill, he practically tripped over his own feet getting down there.

"John!" he shouted. "Ruth! I got food!"

John and Little George peeked through the doorway at him, then stepped outside and waited.

"Food! They gave me food for you!"

Ruth, Margaret and Catherine joined John and Little George. By the time Flattop reached them, he was running so fast and so out of control that he crashed into them, scattering them like bowling pins. He thrust the sacks at John and Ruth, then they all went inside the hut.

Within minutes, the family was tearing at roast beef and gnawing on big chunks of bread. Little George was eating ham from one hand and a cooked carrot from the other. Ruth's eyes got big as saucers when the baked pears were passed around.

Flattop told them how he and William had killed the Robber King and captured his men. John stood to shake his hand and congratulate him. The little girls giggled and asked a million questions about castle life.

For the first time today, Flattop was comfortable. He laughed with them and ate with them, and when Little George crawled onto his lap, he felt like he belonged. When it began to get dark, he helped them clear the dishes and flop the straw mattress onto the table.

They looked at each other in the awkward silence. Finally Flattop said, "Well, I guess I'd better go. They'll wonder where I am."

Ruth and John nodded and thanked him again for the best meal of their lives.

"I'll bring you more food tomorrow," Flattop promised.

John and Ruth exchanged worried glances, then John spoke, "Please, lad . . . we are most grateful for the meal you shared with us tonight, but you must not do this again."

The words stabbed at Flattop's heart. "Why not?"

Ruth answered, "We cannot take food from the castle and—"

"You're not taking it," Flattop said angrily. "I'm giving it to you."

John scratched his head and looked at the ground. "Flattop . . . we must earn our keep. We cannot accept the charity of Lord and Lady Hemstead when we are capable of hard work. A man who depends on others will forget how to use his own hands."

"Yeah, but you could starve," Flattop argued.

"We will work harder." Ruth shrugged her thin shoulders.

Flattop felt the heat rise in his face until he knew he was beet red with anger and embarrassment. Offering help—how stupid could he be? Not accepting it—how stupid could *they* be?

*Fine.*

He wouldn't try again. He mumbled, "I gotta go now," and headed for the door.

As he walked outside, John called after him, "Flattop! Thank you for your kindness. We shall always remember what you did for us tonight."

"Yeah, yeah," Flattop mumbled in a sarcastic whisper. He waved his hand. "See ya."

He tromped back over the hill, angry with everybody. If someone came up to him right now, he'd probably pick a fight with him. "Stupid serfs," he muttered. As he marched down the other side of the hill toward the castle, the dark glass in his pocket jabbed him again. He reached in and pulled it out. "Stupid glass," he grumbled.

The Wizard's face appeared in the purple-y black glass. "My, my. We're cranky tonight."

Flattop was happy to see the Wizard's face again, but he wasn't quite done being mad yet. "Where've you been?"

The Wizard smiled. "Here and there."

"Yeah, well, I talked to a stupid bird all afternoon, thanks to you."

"All afternoon?" The Wizard raised an eyebrow.

"I want to go home," Flattop snapped. "I don't belong here."

The Wizard shook his head. "But Marvin, what about the adventure?"

"I don't have any friends here."

"What about John and Ruth?" the Wizard asked.

"I wanted to bring them more food but they don't want it." Flattop felt a lump growing in his throat that made it hard to swallow.

"They're serfs, my boy. They can't depend on other people to feed them."

"They could depend on me!" Flattop protested.

"And when you go home, what will they do?" The Wizard paused a moment. "Marvin, you have a good heart and I know you want to help. But while on your adventures, you must be careful never to let anyone become dependent on you. You, my boy, are just passing through. Here today, gone tomorrow."

Flattop hadn't thought about it that way. If John and Ruth depended on him to feed them, they really *would* starve when he finally went back home. "So . . ." Flattop asked the Wizard, "I have to help them help themselves?"

"Bingo!" The Wizard winked playfully. "You've got it, my boy."

Just then, William's distant voice could be heard. "Flattop! Flattop, where are you?"

"I believe your *friend* is looking for you." And with that, the Wizard's face faded away.

Flattop called out to William, "Over here!"

William came galloping on horseback. "Where have you been?"

Flattop shrugged. "I needed to take a walk."

"Well," William said, "we may have disposed of the Robber King, but there are other highwaymen out here with robbery—or worse—on their minds. Come." With that, he extended a hand and pulled Flattop onto his horse. The two rode back toward the castle.

After a couple of minutes of silence, Flattop finally spoke. "William?"

"Yes?"

"I'm sorry about leaving the party. It's just that I don't

have any friends here." Flattop looked at William, sitting stick-straight and confident in his saddle. "Do you know what I mean?"

"Aye, Flattop," William replied. "I was fostered out to Lord Hemstead in my seventh winter."

"Fostered?"

William nodded. "My parents, Lord and Lady Wickshire, sent me here to receive my training as a knight. I was taken away from my family and friends to live here. That was ten winters ago."

"Doesn't anyone come to see you?" Flattop asked.

" 'Tis a full day's journey to my family's castle, and I have duties to perform here. However, I look forward to seeing my brother James at my dubbing."

"Aren't your mom and dad coming?" Flattop asked. "I mean, getting dubbed is a pretty big deal, isn't it?"

"Aye. 'Tis an honor I have worked hard to earn." William sighed. "But, alas, my parents are dead. A blight of small pox took the lives of many in my family's castle, including two of my brothers and my only sister."

Flattop felt like a big baby. He had only been away from his family a couple days and he was whining and feeling sorry for himself. William had been sent away ten years ago. He lost his parents, two brothers and a sister, and never even mentioned it until now. *Wimp.* Flattop scolded himself.

They crossed the drawbridge, stabled William's horse and walked up the stairs to the bedchamber. It wasn't long before William started snoring. Flattop smiled. After sleeping with John's entire family, it was nice to have only one other person in the bed.

Flattop fell asleep facedown and fully dressed.

The next morning, Flattop woke up to see William get out of bed and stretch lazily. He thought how nice it was to sleep with someone who was too old to wet the bed—which reminded him, he had to go to the bathroom.

Still lying in bed, he looked at the big clay pot. *Go to the bathroom in there, then let a little girl take it away?* He crinkled up his nose in disgust. His thoughts were interrupted when William grabbed the pot with both hands and took it into the room that held the big tub. Once again, Flattop just wished he could go home. Yesterday he shared William's bath water, today he had to share— He sighed and made a promise to himself to be the first one up tomorrow.

Later, even though he was still tired, he left the bedchamber with William, mostly to avoid that little girl. As they walked down the stairs he smelled hamburgers again, but this time he knew it was the candles. "Does anyone here eat in the morning?" Flattop was trying to find a polite way to say he was starving.

"Aye." William nodded. "You may ask for bread and cheese or fruit at the cookhouse."

"Are you going to eat something?" Flattop asked.

"I cannot. My dubbing is tomorrow morning and I must spend today in fasting and reflection."

"Huh?" was all Flattop could say.

"I must also clean and care for my chain mail and sword."

"So you can't eat?" Flattop didn't get the connection.

"Indeed, I cannot. I shall be thinking about God's purpose for my life and preparing my heart and soul for my vigil tonight."

"So . . . you can't eat tonight, either?"

William turned to Flattop and smiled. "I shall eat at the feast in my honor tomorrow, after I am pronounced Sir William."

Flattop had only gone without food when he had the flu, mainly because he didn't want to throw up. He couldn't imagine someone choosing not to eat for a whole day. "Well," Flattop said, "if you feel dizzy or you start to get a headache, you'd better eat a little something." He remembered his mom saying that once.

William looked both confused and amused at Flattop's advice. He smiled and patted Flattop on the shoulder. "I thank you for your wise counsel."

Flattop nodded. "You're welcome," he replied, even though he had no idea what William had just said.

They walked in silence through the Great Hall, where people were standing on ladders made of sticks and rope, hanging banners, pennants and streamers.

"All is in preparation for the feast tomorrow," William said, smiling.

Just as Flattop and William were about to leave, Flattop felt something shove him from behind. He turned around to see the big, black-and-brown dog nudging him with his nose. He patted the dog on the head. "Hey, boy."

William chuckled. "He likes you."

"What's his name?"

"One of the pages named him Brutus," William answered.

Flattop scratched Brutus behind the ears, and the dog wagged its tail eagerly. William and Flattop left the Great Hall and started down the outside steps of the donjon. Brutus followed, pushing his nose into Flattop's hand, looking for more attention.

At the bottom of the steps, Flattop knelt down, rubbed the dog's muzzle and smiled. "You're a nice boy, aren't you, Bru—" Flattop's mouth dropped open and he stared at the dog's face. *Those eyes. Wise eyes. The Wizard's eyes.*

"Flattop? Are you all right?" William asked.

Flattop couldn't stop staring at the dog. "Uh . . . yeah."

"I must leave you now, Flattop. I have much to do to prepare for tomorrow." William paused. "Will you be all right?"

Flattop nodded, still studying Brutus. "Sure. Go. I've got some stuff to do, too."

"Then, good day, my friend." William headed toward the stables.

Flattop looked deeper into the dog's eyes, but spoke to the Wizard. "I see you in there."

Brutus gave him a wet, sloppy, dog kiss right on the mouth. Flattop sputtered and wiped his jacket sleeve across his face. That's when Brutus took off running.

Flattop chased him all the way to the cookhouse, where workers were throwing scraps of food onto a linen cloth. Brutus gave the cloth a tug, then looked up at Flattop. John's family would consider the pile of fruit peelings and bread crusts to be quite a treat. If only Margaret had a job in the cookhouse. Flattop smiled. Now he knew what he could do to help John's family.

He ran back into the donjon, found Lady Hemstead and asked if Margaret could work in the cookhouse. At first she said she didn't need any more workers, but Flattop reminded her that John's family had helped him recover his strength when his parents were killed. Without the help of

Margaret and her parents, he would never have been able to hunt down the Robber King.

His little lie was turning into a whopper, but he told himself it was for a good cause. Finally Lady Hemstead agreed to let Margaret assist with the preparations for tomorrow's feast. Flattop stuck his fist in the air and yelled, "Yes!" Brutus barked and ran in circles. "We'll go tell Margaret," Flattop said as he and Brutus ran to the door.

"Tell her it is for tomorrow only," Lady Hemstead reminded him.

Flattop and Brutus ran all the way to John's hut, where the family was already hard at work in the fields. "John! Ruth! Margaret's got a job!"

The family gathered around Flattop as he told them about Lady Hemstead's offer. "There's a big feast tomorrow because my friend William's getting dubbed. Lady Hemstead says she'll need more people in the cookhouse, so Margaret gets to work."

John's mouth dropped open, then he let out a hearty laugh. Margaret, Catherine and Little George jumped up and down, squealing with delight.

Only Ruth was quiet. She held her hands over her mouth and stood completely still as tears gathered in her eyes. "Thank you," she whispered. She took a step toward Flattop, rested her hands on either side of his face and said again, "Thank you, son." Then she threw her arms around him and gave him a hug.

"It's only for tomorrow," Flattop reminded them. "But if she's good, maybe they'll keep her."

Ruth nodded and wiped away her tears.

"I will be good," Margaret said, smiling.

A satisfied silence fell over the group. Flattop looked out into the field, then turned to John. "Well, let's get busy."

John smiled and shook his head. "I thank God for you, lad."

The rest of the day was spent in hard work. Even Br
helped by digging furrows with his paws. When the work
was done, Flattop and Brutus walked back to the castle.

Flattop looked down at Brutus. "That was a good idea
about Margaret working in the cookhouse." The dog raised
its brown-and-black head and barked.

Maybe Flattop was just tired, but in his mind he thought
he heard the Wizard's voice say, "It was *your* idea, my boy."

## 22

Dinner at the castle was a lot quieter than the night before. The musicians still played softly next to the big fireplace, but there wasn't any dancing and the dogs didn't jump on the tables. Brutus went off with the brown-and-white dog to snuffle through the rushes on the floor for bones.

Flattop sat at the head table again and talked with Lord and Lady Hemstead. Whenever he could, he slipped in a good word about Margaret. He thanked Lady Hemstead about twenty times for giving the kid a chance. When he was finished eating, he helped the servants clean the tables. Lady Hemstead said it wasn't proper for a noble like Flattop to do scullery work, but he missed pitching in the way he did at home, even though he had to if he wanted his allowance.

With one swipe of his hand, Flattop brushed crumbs and bones onto the floor for the dogs. He used to dream about being a famous baseball player and having a bunch of servants wait on him. But now he felt stupid, sitting around while other people did the work.

It was starting to get dark when he tromped upstairs to his bedchamber. He opened the door to find three men and

three boys surrounding William. They all looked up as Flattop came into the room.

"Hi, William. What's going on?" Flattop asked, hoping he hadn't interrupted some big secret knight thing.

"The time has come, Flattop," William said. "I must prepare for my vigil."

The three young boys walked to the bed and carefully laid out some red, black and white clothes. Flattop remembered when his sister, Marcia, went on her first high school date and her girlfriends laid out different dresses so she could try them on and decide which one didn't make her look fat. But he'd never seen guys do this.

He walked over to the bed to get a closer look. Not only were there clothes on the bed, but there was also a shield, a sword, some spurs and a big clump of metal rings fastened together. He poked at the metal rings. "What's this?"

"That is my mail."

"Oh," Flattop replied, trying to figure out why someone mailed William a bunch of metal rings.

Two of the boys reached across the bed and began fumbling with the metal blob. A few moments later, Flattop recognized what it was. A chain mail tunic and hood, like the knights in movies wore. He picked up the metal tunic. "Whew," he whispered, when he felt how heavy it was.

"That is my *hauberk*," William explained. "As it guards my body, so must I guard the Church," William explained.

"Uh-huh." Flattop nodded, pretending to understand what William meant. He held up the chain mail headpiece. "And this is your hood," he said with some authority.

"My *coif*," William corrected.

"For guarding the church?" Flattop asked.

The boys looked at Flattop, then at each other and smiled. Two of them gathered up the sword, shield, spurs and chain mail, then left.

"Where are they going with your stuff?" Flattop asked.

"To the chapel, where I will perform my vigil," William answered.

The three men led William to the big wooden bathtub, where they helped him undress and get in. They stood around the tub while William scrubbed his face, arms and chest.

The oldest man, who had curly gray hair said, "William of Wickshire, you are cleansed of your blemishes of the past."

William climbed out of the tub, wrapped himself in linen and was escorted to the bed. The remaining boy threw back the covers and William got into bed. Lying on his back with his hands folded over his stomach, he closed his eyes.

The gray-haired man spoke again. "William of Wickshire, you shall know the peaceful sleep God grants his followers, the brave knights." With that, William got out of bed.

Flattop watched intently. This *was* some kind of secret knight thing, after all.

The boy helped William into the white tunic. "This snow white garment," the old man recited, "shall remind you to keep your flesh pure and to devote your life to defending God's law."

Flattop tiptoed to the bed and sat down to watch the rest of the show.

One of the men held out a red robe and William stuck his arms into the sleeves. "This scarlet robe," the gray-haired man said, "means that you are ready to pour out your blood for the Holy Church."

Flattop's mouth dropped open. *Red sleeves mean a Red Sox player has powerful arms. Red stripes, strong legs. Fast of foot. Miles and miles and miles of heart.* The Red Sox had a dressing ceremony just like the knights. Now it didn't seem like such a dumb idea.

The third man helped William into a long, heavy black cloak. "This black cloak," the old man said, "shall serve as a reminder that all men, even you, William of Wickshire, must die."

Flattop shuddered. He was glad Coach Hartman didn't carry the Red Sox dressing ceremony that far.

The attending boy tugged on the bottom of the cloak, making sure it was even. When he was finished, William, the three men and the boy walked to the door of the bedchamber.

"Hey!" Flattop stood up, ready to follow. "Where are you going?"

William stopped and looked back. "To the chapel. I must perform my vigil."

"Can I come?"

"No, Flattop." William turned and walked out the door. "This is my time with God."

Flattop ran to the door and watched them walk down the hall to the stairs. "What time will you be back?"

"I shall not return tonight." Then William turned around one last time and flashed a big, proud grin at Flattop. "I shall see you tomorrow morning at my dubbing. You shall stand with my brother James."

"Okay." Flattop stood in the doorway and tried to look casual as he waved goodbye. "See ya."

Flattop closed the door and looked around the empty room. He couldn't ever remember being this happy for another person. William had worked hard to become a knight, and it meant everything to him. It was probably like winning a million dollars or something.

He walked over to the bed and flopped on top of the covers. It would be nice to meet William's brother in the morning. From what William had told him, James was pretty cool. He was a knight *and* a lord.

Flattop stared at the rich burgundy fabric draped above his head. Funny. He wasn't tired anymore. Just lonely. He tried to whistle something, but lost interest.

Maybe Brutus was still down in the Great Hall. *No harm in checking.* Flattop got up and opened the door. To his surprise, Brutus was sitting right outside.

Flattop knelt down and patted the dog's head. "Hi, boy." But before he could look into the dog's eyes and see if the Wizard was there, Brutus took off down the steps, gleefully wagging his tail.

"Hey! Wait for me!" Flattop shouted, as he hurried down the hall after the brown-and-black dog.

He ran down the steps and practically flew around the corner through the doorway—right into a woman wearing a big black-and-white dress. She stumbled backwards into a table, then landed on the floor.

"Lady Wickshire!" Lady Hemstead's voice rang out. Servants seemed to come from out of nowhere to help her up and dust her off. Flattop's blood ran cold. He'd just blindsided a lady.

"I—I'm sorry," Flattop stammered. "I didn't see you. Honest."

"Flattop Kincaid!" Lady Hemstead's voice had icicles in it. "We shall find a way to deal with your careless behavior."

Flattop wondered if she could order someone to chop off his head, like the queen in *Alice in Wonderland.* He winced as she continued to scold him.

"If you were not a guest of honor in this castle, I would— I would—"

"Please," said Lady Wickshire as she brushed the sticks and leaves from her skirt. "He was not at fault. It was an accident."

"But—but—" Lady Hemstead sputtered, "he came running through here like—like—"

"Like the lad he is." Lady Wickshire smiled. She walked over to Flattop. "Are you all right?"

"Yeah. Are you?" he asked.

"I am well," she said. "So you are the brave orphan, Flattop Kincaid. My husband's brother, William of Wickshire, has been your companion of late."

*Holy cow!* Flattop thought to himself. *I tackled William's sister-in-law!*

"I am Lady Wickshire. However, since I feel I know you, please call me Alice." She held out her hand to him. Flattop started to shake her hand, then figured he was probably supposed to kiss it instead. So he did.

She laughed. A warm, loving, everything-will-be-okay laugh. She turned to Lady Hemstead and winked. "Can such a gentleman as this be punished for an accident?"

Lady Hemstead clapped her hands twice and directed the servants to bring Alice some supper.

"Please," Alice interrupted. "I always enjoy the cookhouse. I shall fetch something for myself."

Lady Hemstead ordered a young boy to show Alice to the kitchen, but Alice said, "Flattop can escort me. I want to talk to this young noble who faced death so bravely."

Alice and Lady Hemstead were both looking at him, so he figured he'd better say something. "Sure. I'm not doing anything right now." He started across the Great Hall, then looked back to see if she was following. "C'mon."

Alice laughed softly. "As you wish, sir." She turned to Lady Hemstead. "I thank you again for your kind hospitality, Lady Hemstead. You are a generous and gracious hostess." She caught up with Flattop just as he opened the door to the outside steps of the donjon.

Lady Hemstead called out a stern warning, "And *no* running."

"I shall try not to," Alice answered, winking playfully at Flattop.

# 23

Sitting in the cookhouse, laughing and talking with Alice, Flattop felt warm and comfortable. She was such a . . . well, she was like a mom. She asked him about his family, his home and his baseball uniform. Flattop stuck to the same story he'd told everyone else, but what he really wanted to do was tell her the truth. He felt safe with her.

Alice wasn't really, *really* old. She was twenty-four winters, as she put it. She had light green eyes that were the color of Flattop's best cat's-eye marble. And when she smiled, her whole face smiled.

"It pleases me, Flattop," she said, "that our William has found himself such a good and true friend."

Flattop felt his cheeks tingle and he knew his face must be bright red. "William's pretty cool, too."

"I believe Fortune smiled on both of you," she said, as she nibbled on a piece of baked apple. "Friendship is a gift from God." She looked sad as she picked at the oven-browned peel.

"I've got lots of friends back home." Flattop hoped he

could get her to smile again. "This one kid, Jason, can sing 'Happy Birthday' in one belch."

"Oh, my."

Flattop chuckled just thinking about it. "Yeah. It's pretty funny," he said, nodding. When he noticed that she wasn't laughing he added, "At least, it's funny where I come from."

"Is there no chivalry in California?" Alice asked.

"Huh?"

"A code of honor," she explained. "Rules that tell nobles how to behave."

"We've got manners," Flattop replied. "Like, 'Don't talk with your mouth full.' Stuff like that."

"Aye. And your . . . manners . . . allow a young noble to belch and sing at the same time?"

"Heck, no." Flattop laughed. "If you did that around an adult, they'd have a cow."

"I see," said Alice, though Flattop could tell she didn't.

He decided to change the subject. "So, where's James?"

"My husband?"

"Yeah. William said I get to stand with him tomorrow."

Alice sighed, then shifted uncomfortably in her chair. "Lord Wickshire could not break from his duties. He sent me to represent him and to bid William return to our lands. My husband looks forward to acquiring another knight."

Suddenly sweet ol' Alice was sounding like one of those politicians on the news who has to go to a foreign country when there's a funeral.

She pushed away her plate. "I have not the appetite for this."

Flattop crinkled up his nose. "Yeah. I don't like baked apples either. I like 'em raw."

Alice looked at him and gasped. "Flattop, you cannot mean you would eat an apple uncooked!"

"Yeah." Flattop shrugged. "What's the big deal? Everyone gets hyper about fresh fruit around here."

"All fruit must be cooked. Otherwise, it is poisonous," Alice warned.

Flattop jumped up from his chair. "It is not." He walked over to a basket of apples and grabbed one. "Here, I'll show you." He raised the apple to take a bite.

"Flattop, no!" Alice jumped up from her chair, then winced, grabbed her stomach and sat back down.

Flattop dropped the apple back into the basket. "What's wrong?"

" 'Tis my child," she said.

For the first time, Flattop noticed that underneath all those puffy black and white clothes, Alice was very pregnant. And Flattop was very nervous. "You're not having a baby *now,* are you?"

Alice smiled and shook her head. "No, lad. But I have had a long journey and I must get some rest." She placed both hands on the big wooden chopping table and slowly stood up. "I must go to bed."

Flattop walked her all the way to her chamber door, praying that she wouldn't decide to have the baby right there. When her door closed, he leaned against the stone wall and breathed a sigh of relief.

He started toward his own bedchamber, then realized William probably didn't know Alice had arrived. He decided to go to the chapel and tell him so he wouldn't worry.

The night was so quiet that Flattop could hear the *click-clunk* of his baseball cleats echo off the high walls around him. The chill in the night air, plus the spooky quiet, made him feel a little cold. He pulled his cap tighter onto his head, shoved his hands deep into the pockets of his red satin jacket and hunched his shoulders.

The chapel door was not quite shut, and a faint, warm light spilled through the opening. Flattop slowly pushed the door open and peeked in. William was kneeling at the altar before a single flickering candle. His black cloak fell in folds behind him. Flattop whispered, "William?"

William turned around slowly and whispered back, "Flattop?"

Flattop walked up the narrow aisle as quietly as he could. "I just wanted to tell you Alice is here."

William grinned. "She traveled with my brother, then?"

"No, he couldn't come."

William sat back on his heels, looking disappointed. "I see."

"He really wanted to, but he was . . . busy." Just saying the words made Flattop realize what a dumb excuse it was. After all, getting dubbed was a once-in-a-lifetime thing.

William nodded, then squared his shoulders and turned to face the altar again. "My brother must oversee his lands. It is a heavy burden." He folded his hands and bowed his head again.

*Way to go,* Flattop thought to himself. *Now he's depressed.* He decided to change the subject. "So . . ." he started, then looked around the chapel, "this is a vigil, huh?"

"Aye," William replied.

Flattop looked at the burning candle. It cast dancing shadows on the sword, spurs, shield and chain mail that lay on the altar beside it. "Hey, look," he said as he walked up to the altar. "Here's all your stuff."

"Aye," William said again.

"So . . . are you praying about your stuff?"

William looked at Flattop. "My . . . *stuff* . . . is my reminder of my life's mission."

"Huh?"

William rested his hand on his shield. "This reminds me that I must protect the Holy Church." He ran his hand along the smooth, polished surface of his sword. "My weapon has two edges, which means I serve God and His people." He lightly touched the tip and smiled. "And the point reminds *them* to obey *me*."

Flattop gave a long, low whistle. "How do you remember all this?"

"I have been schooled in the responsibilities of knighthood since the day I was born. My duty is to honor God, serve the Church and protect Man."

Flattop frowned. "Doesn't sound like much fun."

" 'Tis my calling," was all William said, then once again folded his hands and bowed his head.

Flattop traced a crack in the stone flooring with the tip of his baseball cleat. "Yeah, well . . . I'd better go." He walked back down the aisle and pushed the door open.

"Flattop?"

"Yeah?" Flattop looked over his shoulder at William, who was still facing the altar.

"Thank you for telling me of Alice's arrival. I shall see you both tomorrow."

Flattop nodded. "Sure. No problem."

He walked down the alley to the donjon and up the stairs. This knight stuff wasn't anything like what he'd seen in the movies. Come to think of it, nothing around here was like the movies.

He scratched an itch on his shoulder, then one on his leg. Lice again. Or maybe it was fleas. Even the rich people had them. He'd have to take a bath in the morning before the dubbing. He didn't want to stand next to Alice and scratch like an old dog.

When he opened the heavy wooden door, Brutus was on the other side, waiting. The big dog jumped up and rested his paws on Flattop's chest, almost knocking him back down the steps.

"Whoa, boy," Flattop said. He tried to look into the dog's eyes again, but Brutus just kept slurping Flattop's face with those wet dog kisses.

Flattop finally pushed the dog off his chest. "Come on, Brutus." He smiled and scratched behind the dog's ears, then walked to his bedchamber with Brutus following close behind.

"Hey, Brutus. You wouldn't happen to have a couple flea collars, would you?"

# 24

The morning of William's dubbing dawned with a flurry of activity. Servants filled Flattop's bathtub with buckets of water while he played with Brutus. Flattop had forgotten about the little girl who collected the chamber pot. When she showed up, he was so embarrassed he pretended he had something important to do and left the room.

When he returned for a long soak in his lukewarm bath, he was grateful that he didn't have to share his bath water with anyone today. He put on his baseball uniform with a prouder feeling about Coach Hartman's dressing ceremony, but he was a little uncomfortable about wearing a Red Sox uniform to something as important as a dubbing. He threw on his jacket, pulled his cap down to his forehead and ran out the door, with Brutus tagging along.

Flattop peeked in at the chapel to see how the vigil was going, but when he saw Lord Hemstead, Sir Humphrey and a priest praying with William, he decided to eat breakfast instead.

In the cookhouse, two big-muscled men hacked away at the hindquarters of a deer, while others roasted ham and beef over the fiery, hissing grill. Women cut up vegetables and threw them by handfuls into blackened metal stewpots, then struggled together to lift the pots onto hooks in the roaring fireplace. Teenagers and kids sliced fruit for baking and chopped up chickens for boiling. In the middle of it all was Lady Hemstead, tasting sauces and giving orders.

Flattop wanted something to eat, but he remembered one Thanksgiving morning when he walked into his own kitchen and asked for a bowl of Cheerios. Even his grandmother yelled at him. There was no telling what Lady Hemstead might do.

He turned to leave and bumped right into Alice—only this time he didn't knock her down.

"Good morning, Flattop," she said in a cheery voice. "Have you eaten?"

"No." He shook his head then looked back at all the frantic workers. "But I can wait."

Alice put her arm around his shoulder. "Nonsense, boy. Come with me." She led him back into the cookhouse, then calmly made her way through the chaos to cut a chunk of white cheese off a bulky, round slab. She pulled a chair away from the chopping table and scooted it over, next to the door. "Sit down."

"Thanks." He took the cheese and bit off a big hunk.

"I have sent a girl to the bakery to fetch some bread. She should returned presently." Alice looked out the door. "Ah, here she is."

Flattop looked up to see Margaret walk through the door, her arms full of fresh bread. He stood up. "Margaret!"

"Flattop!" Margaret smiled the biggest smile he'd ever seen.

Alice raised her eyebrows. "You know each other?"

"Aye, my lady. 'Tis Flattop who got me the chance to work here today."

Flattop looked at Alice. "Margaret's family took care of

me when my—when I first got here." Funny. He didn't want to keep the orphan lie going in front of Alice.

"Well, then," Alice said, "she is very special, indeed." She took a loaf of bread from Margaret's arms, tore off the end and handed it to Flattop.

Flattop looked at it, then at Margaret. "Here," he said, handing the bread to her. "I'm not very hungry."

Margaret stepped back, wide-eyed, and shook her head. "I cannot take food from Lady Hemstead's cookhouse. I must work hard to prove myself."

"Yes, you must, child," Alice said. "Now run along. Flattop and I must be leaving."

Margaret gave a quick curtsy, then scurried to the other side of the cookhouse, presented the bread to Lady Hemstead and curtsied again.

"She's hungry," Flattop protested.

"Aye." Alice nodded. "But she will be dismissed if she steals food." She motioned for Flattop to follow her, then walked out the door and through the alley to the inner drawbridge.

"Margaret wasn't stealing. I was *giving* it to her."

Alice shook her head. "She is a serf, Flattop. She cannot eat food that is meant for a noble, even if you offer it to her. Do you wish her to keep this job?"

"Yeah."

"Then you must not tempt her," Alice warned.

Flattop sighed. He'd never understand the Middle Ages.

Alice put her hand on his shoulder and smiled. "Come. We will go to the courtyard for William's dubbing. And while we wait, you shall tell me more of your California."

Flattop and Alice sat on a wooden bench in the empty courtyard. He told her about his home, his friends, his school and even his sister. Of course, he tried to make it sound as Middle Age-y as possible. He stayed away from

146

the subject of his mom and dad because he didn't want to lie to Alice.

Slowly the courtyard filled with children and adults, but Flattop kept talking. He was in the middle of telling Alice about the Red Sox when she nodded toward the courtyard entrance and stood up.

Lord Hemstead, Sir Humphrey and the priest entered, looking very solemn. Behind them came William, walking proudly in his white tunic, red robe and black cloak. The three boys who had been part of William's dressing ceremony entered next. One boy carried William's sword and the other two carried spurs. Flattop stood at attention as they walked past.

First, the priest said a prayer about William obeying God's commands, then Lord Hemstead gave a speech about William's loyalty and dedication to duty. Then he praised William for bravely killing the Robber King.

The whole ceremony reminded Flattop of his cousin Nancy's wedding. Both had a formal procession down the aisle with the audience standing up, though Nancy had a ring bearer and William had sword-and-spur bearers. Now Lord Hemstead was talking to William the way the minister had talked to Nancy and her groom. The speech was directed at William, but everyone else was supposed to pay attention.

Lord Hemstead told William that his horse was a symbol of all the people who must support him and do what he says. "As a knight guides his horse, so you must guide your people."

Then William promised to obey the *code of chivalry*. Flattop remembered that *chivalry* meant you couldn't burp and sing "Happy Birthday" at the same time.

William swore he would stop all villains and thieves and defend and protect all widows and orphans. *Orphans*. Maybe that's why William was always so nice to Flattop. A twinge of guilt over the lies he'd told formed a small knot in his stomach.

The three boys stepped forward. The first two attached the spurs to William's shoes. The third presented the sword, dangling from a leather belt, to Lord Hemstead.

"Knights must have two hearts," Lord Hemstead continued, as he fastened the sword around William's waist. "One as hard as a diamond, the other as soft as warm wax. Use the hard heart against traitors, and the soft heart for those in need."

William knelt in front of Lord Hemstead, and the priest said another prayer. Flattop added a couple of silent prayers about his family back home. First, he said one for his dad, who was always saying that boys Flattop's age should go out and have real adventures instead of playing video games. Then he said a prayer for his mom, who was always worried that he was going to hurt himself if he wasn't careful.

Flattop wondered what his parents would say if they knew what he'd been through in the Middle Ages. His dad would probably shake his head and ask him a million questions. His mom would probably cry for a couple hours and keep saying, "Thank goodness you're all right."

When the priest finished his prayers, Flattop opened his eyes to see Lord Hemstead take a step toward William. In a loud voice, he said, "I pronounce you *Sir* William of Wickshire. Receive this in remembrance of God, who ordained you, and of me, who dubbed you." With that, he raised his hand and smacked William as hard as he could on the side of the head. Flattop gasped as William toppled to the ground.

Alice placed a calming hand on Flattop's arm.

Lord Hemstead reached down and offered his hand to William to help him stand up again. "That, Sir William, is the last blow that shall go unanswered."

148

All the men applauded and the women waved handkerchiefs and scarves. Flattop rubbed the side of his head out of sympathy for William.

"Come," Alice said. "Let us prepare to meet Sir William in the Great Hall."

Flattop looked at the swarm of people surrounding his friend and nodded. It would be impossible to get within five feet of him now. He walked with Alice toward the donjon steps.

"Why did Lord Hemstead have to hit him like that?" Flattop asked.

Alice turned to him. "Do you mean the *colee?* The blow to the head?"

"He practically knocked William's head off."

Alice smiled. " 'Tis a tradition. A knight is a warrior—a battler. The colee announces to all who witness it that, from this day forward, any man who strikes William shall pay for it with his life."

"Well, I think Lord Hemstead is taking a pretty stupid chance. What if he broke William's jaw or something?"

Alice scowled. "I find it odd that the young man who talks of eating uncooked, poisonous apples would feel so strongly about taking *stupid chances.*"

"But I told you, apples aren't—" He stopped in mid-defense when he saw the mischievous twinkle in Alice's eyes. "Okay, you win," he said, smiling.

He helped Alice up the steps to the Great Hall, opened the door for her, then told her he'd be right back. He turned and ran down the stairs, through the alley and into the cookhouse. After giving Margaret a smile and a little wave, he scrunched between the workers to get to the basket of apples sitting in the far corner.

*I'll show her.* Flattop smiled to himself. He stuffed the apple into the pocket of his jacket and ran back through the alley, imagining Alice's surprise and delight when he ate a fresh apple and didn't die. The thought of his upcoming victory in the poison-apple issue made him run even faster. By the time he rounded the corner, he felt like he was going about sixty miles an hour.

That's when he plowed right into the hunched-over figure in the grayish black cloak and the two of them tumbled to the ground.

Flattop sat up, dazed. He hoped he had run into a serf. If he knocked over another noble, Lady Hemstead would probably scream her head off.

He tried to get a better look at his victim. The hood of the cloak completely covered the other person's face, and he didn't know if he had knocked down a man or a woman. He watched the mysterious figure get up on hands and knees.

"I'm sorry. I didn't know you were there," Flattop said.

"That's all right, Marvin, my boy," a familiar voice said from under the floppy hood. "It's one of the hazards of the game."

Flattop saw a flash of purple robe under the long cloak and gasped. "It's you!" He grabbed the hem of the Wizard's robe and held on tight. "I caught you!"

## 25

The Wizard sat on the cobblestones in the alley, pulled the hood away from his face and sighed. "*Caught* me? You nearly *killed* me."

Flattop laughed, then crawled next to the white-haired old man and sat down. "I said I was sorry."

"Well, my boy, you won the game," the Wizard sighed. "Are you ready to go home?"

"Yeah!" Then Flattop thought about William and Alice, and the big feast. "Wait! I mean—can I have a little more time?"

The Wizard looked Flattop right in the eye, then nodded and started to get up. "Sure, Marvin, my boy. All you have to do is catch me again."

Flattop clutched the Wizard's arm and held on. "Wait! No."

The Wizard sat down again with a sigh. "Well then, make up your mind."

Flattop scrambled for an answer while keeping a death grip on the Wizard's arm.

"May I have your answer before my arm falls off?" the Wizard grumbled.

"Okay," said Flattop, reaching into his back pocket for the dark glass. "I'll go home." Just saying the words brought back a flood of memories: his mom and dad, his sister, friends, the Red Sox, school.

It was time.

He touched the glass to the Wizard's hand, prepared for the purple lightning flashes and the deafening sound of his own heartbeat. But it didn't happen. His head simply fell forward and he heard a distant *tap, tap, tap.*

*Tap, tap, tap.*

"Flattop?" His mother's voice reached into his brain and woke him up.

*Tap, tap, tap.*

Flattop opened his eyes and raised his head. He was sitting at his very own computer in his very own bedroom.

"Marvin, honey?" *Tap, tap, tap.* His very own mother was knocking on his bedroom door.

He rubbed his eyes. "Yeah, Mom. Come in."

The door opened slowly and there stood his mom holding a lunch tray of soup, crackers and a big glass of milk. She looked so beautiful, he just kept staring at her.

"What's the matter?" she asked.

Even though he missed her and was happy to see her again, he couldn't get all mushy and tell her that. So he just said, "You're wearing your jeans."

His mother looked down, then leaned her shoulder against the doorway. "Yeah . . . is there something wrong with them?"

"No." Flattop took off his hat and ran his fingers through his hair. "It's just that I haven't seen any jeans for a long time."

Her brow furrowed. "Oh." She walked into the room and put the tray of food on his desk, next to the computer. "Here you go, honey. This'll make you feel better."

Flattop stared at the food. "Mom? Did you and dad miss me . . . lately?"

"Miss you?"

"I mean . . . did you know I was gone for a while?"

"When?"

"Just now. I saw a guy become a knight."

His mom smiled, then put her hands on his shoulders. "Sounds like you took a little nap."

Flattop had to admit his brain was fuzzy, just like it usually felt when he fell asleep on the couch for a couple hours. He stared at the computer screen, where a cartoon wizard in a purple robe stood motionless.

"Did you?" his mom asked.

"Huh?" He rubbed his eyes again, trying to get them to focus better.

"Did you take a nap?" Her voice sounded a little worried.

Flattop looked at his uniform. There were no signs of the dirt and smoke of the Middle Ages. He rubbed his thumb along the edge of the dark glass in his hand, then he stared at the cartoon wizard on the computer screen again.

"Yeah," he said, clearing his throat. "I guess I fell asleep."

"Well, eat your soup, then take a shower and crawl into that bed, young man. You have school tomorrow and I don't want you getting sick. It's the end of the school year and you have a lot of tests to study for, so . . ."

She was lecturing him, all right. But it sounded great. So did a shower. So did a bed with an actual mattress. One he wouldn't have to share with a squire who snored or a little kid who wet the bed.

And he had school tomorrow. Something a smart girl like Margaret would never get to experience. He'd never have believed he'd think something like this, but he felt lucky to be born at a time when kids *had* to go to school.

"Did you hear me, Marvin?" his mother asked.

"Yeah. Okay, Mom." He hadn't heard much of what she

153

had to say, but his answer seemed to satisfy her. He watched her walk toward his bedroom door. "Hey, Mom?"

She turned around and gave one of those disgusted-mom sighs. "Yes?"

"Thanks . . . okay?" He hoped she understood that a kid just couldn't say the kinds of things he was feeling.

"Thanks?" She studied him carefully, then her gaze moved to the tray of food she'd brought in. "Oh. You're welcome, honey." She walked out, closing his bedroom door.

Flattop smelled the aroma of steamy chicken noodle soup. "This is better than porridge, any day," he mumbled to himself. He looked at the cartoon wizard frozen in place on the computer monitor.

"What a dream," he said with a smile. Alice, William, John and Ruth, the Robber King. He hoped Margaret got to keep her castle job. Then he laughed at himself. *Keep her job? It was a dream!*

He crumbled some crackers into his soup bowl, then started to take off his jacket. That's when he felt the lump in his pocket. He reached in and pulled out a round, fresh, red apple. He stared in amazement at the apple, then looked at the computer screen.

The Wizard smiled and winked. "You won this round fair and square, my boy. Care to play another?"